# THE DANGER
# THAT LURKS
# WITHIN

## Ernest Morris

**GOOD 2 GO PUBLISHING**

**THE DANGER THAT LURKS WITHIN**
Written by Ernest Morris
Cover Design: Davida Baldwin, Odd Ball Designs
Typesetter: Mychea
ISBN: 978-1-947340-68-8
Copyright © 2021 Good2Go Publishing
Published 2021 by Good2Go Publishing
7311 W. Glass Lane • Laveen, AZ 85339
www.good2gopublishing.com
https://twitter.com/good2gobooks
G2G@good2gopublishing.com
www.facebook.com/good2gopublishing
www.instagram.com/good2gopublishing

# Chapter 1

Sharon Stone was thirty minutes into her morning exercise and breathing hard as she ran south along a path by the Tidal Basin in Washington, DC. It was a gorgeous spring day in late March, warm with a fragrant breeze. The trees that lined the path were in full bloom, attracting early birds. Sharon had to dodge a few people who were also out getting their morning jog in, but it was so nice of a day that she didn't mind.

She was in her late thirties, but her legs felt stronger than they had when she was just out of college, so did her breathing, and that pleased her. The daily exercise was working. Leaving the Tidal Basin, Sharon cut past the statue of John Jones and jogged in place, waiting to cross Seventeenth Street SE beside a

DC bus discharging and loading passengers.

When the bus sighed and rolled away, Sharon looped around the pedestrians to cross the street, toward the National Sylvan Theater and another grove of blooming cherry trees. The cherry blossoms only peaked once a year, and she intended to enjoy them as much as possible. She'd just passed a knot of Japanese tourists when her cell phone rang.

She plucked the phone from the small fanny pack she wore, but did not stop or slow. Sharon glanced at the unfamiliar phone number and let her voicemail take the call. She ran on and soon could see a team of National Park Police raising flags surrounding the base of the Washington Monument. Her phone rang again, same number.

Irritated, she stopped and answered, "Sharon Stone."

"Chief Sharon Stone?"

The voice was male. Or was it? The tone wasn't deep.

"Who's calling, please?"

"Your worst nightmare, Chief. There's an IED on the National Mall. You should have answered my first call. Now you only have fifty-eight minutes to figure out where I left it."

The line went dead. Sharon stared at the phone half a beat, then checked her watch: 7:28 a.m. Detonation would be 8:26 a.m.? She hit a number on speed dial and surveyed the area, swallowing the impulse to get well off the Mall as fast as possible. DC Metro Police Chief Jim Probes answered on the second ring.

"Why is my chief of detectives calling me? I told her to take a few days off."

"I just got an anonymous call, Jim," Sharon said. "An IED planted on the National Mall, set to go off at 8:26 a.m. We need to clear the area as fast as possible and bring in the dogs."

In the short silence that followed, Sharon thought of something and started sprinting toward the men raising flags.

"Are you sure it wasn't a crank?" Chief Probes asked.

"Do you want to take the chance it isn't a prank?"

Probes let out a sharp puff of breath and said, "I'll notify National Park and Capitol Hill Police. You sound like you're running. Where are you?"

"On the Mall. Going to high ground to spot the bomber on his way out of Dodge."

~ ~ ~

It was 7:36 a.m. when the elevator doors opened. Sharon rushed out onto the observation platform of the Washington Monument, some 554 feet above the National Mall. She carried a chattering US Park Service Police radio, tuned to a frequency being used by all FBI, US Capitol Police, and DC Metro Police personnel rapidly responding to the situation.

She had a pair of binoculars lent to her by the officers guarding the closed monument. Balking at her initial demand to be let in, they had given her a hard time while checking her story. Then the sirens had started wailing from all angles, and their commander came back with direct orders to open the monument and let her ride to the top. Sharon had lost eight minutes in the process, but pushed that frustration to the back of her mind.

They had fifty minutes to find the bomb. Sharon went straight to the high slit windows cut in the west wall of the monument and peered through the binoculars toward the Lincoln

Memorial and the long, rectangular pool that reflected its image and that of the Wash-ington Monument. When she'd started to run toward the towering limestone obelisk, she'd hoped to get high enough to catch sight of someone fleeing the Mall or acting strangely.

But too much time had passed. The bomber would have beat feet, gotten as far away as possible, wouldn't he? That was the logical thought, but Sharon wondered if he might be the kind of sicko to stick around, admire his explosive handiwork.

Even at this early hour there were scores of people running, walking, and riding on the paths that crisscrossed the Mall and paralleled the reflecting pool. Others were standing as if transfixed by the chorus of sirens coming closer and closer. Sharon pivoted, strode across the observation deck to the east wall where she could look out toward the US Capitol, and triggered the radio mic.

"This is Metro CoD Stone," she said, scanning the open park between the Smithsonian museums. "I can see hundreds of people still on the mall, and who knows how many more that I can't see because of the trees. Move officers to Seventeenth, Fifteenth, Madison Drive Northwest, Jefferson Drive Southwest, Ohio Drive Southwest, and Seventh Northwest, Fourth Northwest, and Third Northwest. Work civilian evacuation from the middle of the mall to the north and south. Keep it quick and orderly. We don't want to cause panic."

"Roger that, Chief," said the dispatcher.

Sharon grew up in Philadelphia. She moved away to Washington for college, because she wanted to get out of there. She studied journalism and wanted to be a great reporter someday.

When her parents died in a home evasion, she decided to change occupations and become a cop. Since she was still living in Washington, she joined their force.

She waited until she heard the dispatcher call out her orders, then said, "Block all traffic through the Mall north and south and Constitution and Independence Avenues from Third to Ohio."

"That's already been ordered, Chief," the dispatcher said.

"Status of K-9 and bomb squads?"

"FBI, Metro, and Park Police K-9's en route, but traffic's snarling. Metro's ETA on Fifteenth is two minutes. Bomb squads say five minutes out, but could be longer."

Longer? She cursed inwardly. She looked down at the flags fluttering and noted their direction and stiffness. She triggered the mic again.

"Tell K-9 patrols that the wind here is south-southwest, maybe ten miles an hour. They'll want to work from northeast angles."

"Roger that," the dispatcher said.

Sharon checked her watch. 7:41. They had forty-five minutes to find and defuse the IED. Gazing out, her mind racing, Sharon realized she knew something about the bomber. He or she had used the term IED, Improvised Explosive Device, not bomb. IED was a military term. Was the bomber ex-military? Current military?

Then again, Sharon had seen and heard the term often enough on news and media reports. But why would a civilian use that term instead of bomb? Why be so specific about it? Her phone rang. Chief Probes.

"Because of your unique location and perspective, we're giving you overall command of the situation, Chief," he said by way of greeting. "K-9, bomb, and tactical squads will operate at your call after advising you of the option."

Sharon didn't miss a beat. "FBI and Capitol Hill?"

"Waiting on your orders."

"Thank you for the confidence, sir."

"Prove it," he said, and hung up.

For the next six minutes, as she monitored radio chatter, Sharon roamed back and forth, looking east and west, seeing cruiser after cruiser turn sideways to block access to Constitution and Independence Avenues where they ran parallel to the Mall.

At 7:49, twenty-one minutes after the bomber's phone call, mounted police appeared and cantered their horses the length of the Mall, shouting to everyone to leave the quickest way possible. Other patrol cars cruised Independence, Constitution, and Madison, using their bullhorns to spur the evacuation.

Despite Sharon's hope for calm, the police horses and bullhorns were clearly seeding panic. Joggers turned and sprinted north and south off the Mall. Fathers grabbed their kids and ran. Moms pushed baby carriages helter-skelter. Tourists poured like ants out of the Lincoln Memorial and left the Vietnam and World War II Memorials in droves.

Sharon kept the binoculars pressed tight to her eyes, looking for someone lingering, someone wanting a last look at the spot where the bomb was stashed, or positioned to remotely detonate the device. But she saw no one that set off alarm bells. "The son of a bitch is gone," she thought. "Long gone."

# Chapter 2

The bomb dogs did not appear until 7:59 a.m., delayed by traffic caused by closing the Mall during rush hour. They had twenty-seven minutes to find the device, and Sharon was fighting off a panic that threatened to freeze her. She was in charge. What if something went wrong? What I the device went off?

As quickly as the question popped into her mind, Sharon squashed it. The officers and agents convening on the Mall were outstanding, the best. "You're leading superior people," she thought. "Trust them to do their jobs and advise you well, and you'll be confident in your decisions."

The Mall was almost empty when handlers released twelve German shepherds at intervals along Constitution Avenue from the west lawn of the Capitol to the Lincoln Memorial. Sharon watched the dogs roam into the wind in big loops, noses up, sniffing out scents as their handlers tried to keep pace.

A minute passed, and then two. On the radio, bomb squad leaders from the four law enforcement agencies announced their team's arrivals at positions along Independence Avenue, now empty save for cruisers with blue lights flashing.

At 8:02, Sharon was looking west toward the Capitol when one of the FBI's shepherds slowed, circled, and then sat by a trash bin along a pathway west of Seventh Street, almost directly south of the National Sculpture Museum.

"K-9 Pablo says he's got a package," the dog's handler said over the radio.

Sharon closed her eyes. They'd found it with what, twenty-five minutes to spare?

"Back K-9 Pablo off," Sharon said. "Bomb squads move to his location."

The FBI and Capitol Hill Police bomb squads were closest. Tactical vans raced east along Monroe from Third and west from Fifteenth, stopping a block away from the trash bin at 8:04. They had twenty-two minutes to neutralize the threat.

Agents and officers in full bomb gear piled out of vans. Two FBI bomb experts walked within fifty yards of the trash can before releasing an Andros Mark V-A1, a four-wheel-drive robot that rolled right up next to it bearing electronic sensors and cameras.

"We have a time device," one of the agents said, within seconds. "Repeat, we have a time device."

"Evidence of cellular linkage?" another radio-ed back.

"Negative."

Special agent Peggy Denton, the FBI bomb squad commander, called for heavy mats and blankets made of fire-retardant Nomex materials stuffed with sliced-up tire rubber. Four agents and five Capitol Hill police officers carried the mats and blankets toward the trash can.

Sharon's breath caught in her throat when they got within ten feet. If the bomber had a remote trigger on the IED, which was not cell phone driven.

But without hesitation, the bomb team showed exceptional courage. They went to the trash can and laid two bomb mats over it, and then a bomb blanket that draped over the entire can down to the sidewalk. The agents and officers moved back quickly, yanking off their hooded visors, and Sharon sighed with relief. It was 8:11. Fifteen minutes to spare.

"Job well done," Sharon said into the radio, suddenly feeling weak and tired.

She sat down against the wall and closed her eyes, her fingers playing with her wedding ring, an old habit, until she thought to call her husband, E. J. She not only wanted, but also needed to hear his voice. After four rings, she realized that he was probably with a patient.

"E. J. Morris," his voicemail said. "Leave your message at the beep."

"Hey, baby," she said, fighting down a surge of emotion. "I'm okay. I was running on the Mall and —."

Her radio squawked. "Command, this is Metro K-9 Handler Krause. K-9 Rebel has alerted. Exterior trash bin, women's public restroom immediately southwest of Constitution Gardens Pond."

"Shit," Sharon said, getting on her feet and

running to the opposite window as she ordered the officer and his dog back. She saw them trotting north toward open ground and heard the sirens of the other two bomb squads rushing to the new site.

Were there more IEDs? Sharon wondered. All set to go off at 8:26? It was 8:18 as the tactical vans skidded to a stop well back from the restroom. If the bomb was timed to go off at 8:26, they had eight minutes. As before, officers and agents in heavy protective gear and visors poured out of the vans. There was brief radio chatter regarding tactics before Denton spoke.

"Command, I recommend we move straight to the bomb mats and blankets. No time for the robots."

"No other options?" Sharon said.

"We let it blow."

9:19. Seven minutes.

"Mats and blankets," Sharon said. She now spotted police and news helicopters hovering outside the no-fly zone covering much of the Mall and all of the White House grounds to the north.

"Command, we have a Caucasian male in camouflage gear on the west Mall," an officer called.

Sharon swung the binoculars and spotted him. The man was wearing filthy military desert fatigues, dancing in circles and shouting at the sky, on the lawn north of the Ash Woods. Officers ran toward him, shouting at him to get down. Sharon focused her binoculars on the man. Tall, lanky, bearded, and grimy, with matted dark hair and wild eyes, he saw them coming and took off toward the reflecting pool.

Before they could catch him he darted

through the trees and across a path and jumped into the pool. He waded fast toward the center of the pool, heading almost directly toward the bomb squads and the restrooms. The water was well above his knees when he stopped, reached into his pants pocket, and slipped out a Glock pistol.

"Gun!" she barked into the radio. "Repeat, suspect in reflecting pool is armed and dangerous."

The police and FBI agents closing on the pool all had their weapons drawn now, shouting at the man to drop his pistol even as the bomb teams approached the restrooms north of the reflecting pool. The man ignored the warnings. He sat down in the water, which came up to his chest. Holding the Glock overhead, he released the clip, which fell and disappeared below the surface.

He ran the action next and ejected the round from the chamber before expertly stripping the weapon down to its components. Every bit of the gun was in pieces and sunk in under thirty seconds. The officers were in the pool with him now, wading toward him, training their weapons on him, when he flopped back and disappeared into the water.

"What the hell is that guy doing?" Sharon thought. She turned her attention back to the restroom and the first four members of the bomb squad who were close, maybe twelve feet from the second trash can, preparing to lay down the first mat. She glanced at her watch: 8:23. Three minutes to spare.

She exhaled with relief as the bomb experts lifted the mat over the can and the IED exploded in a brilliant, fiery red and yellow flash.

# Chapter 3

Thirty-four-year-old Kate Williams was curled up in the fetal position in the overstuffed chair opposite me, in the basement office where I'd been seeing patients since being suspended from DC Metro five months before.

"I'll end up killing myself, Dr. Morris," Kate said. "Probably not today or tomorrow, but it's going to happen soon. I've known that since I was nine years old."

Her voice was flat, her expression showing the anger, fear, and despair that her tone didn't betray. Tears welled and slipped from eyes that would not meet mine. I took her threat seriously. From her records, I knew some of the damage she'd done to herself already. Kate's teeth were stained from drug abuse. Her dirty blond hair was as thin and brittle as straw, and she wore a long-sleeve Electric Daisy Carnival T-shirt to hide evidence of cutting.

"Is that when it started?" I asked. "When you were nine?"

Kate wiped her eyes furiously. "You know, I'm not talking about it anymore. Digging around back there never helps. Just pushes me to pull the plug on sobriety, on everything, sooner."

I set my notepad aside, sat forward with my palms up, and said, "I'm just trying to understand your history clearly, Kate."

She crossed her arms. "And I'm just trying to hang on, Doc. The court ordered me here as a term of my probation. Otherwise, I gotta tell you, I'd be a no-show."

This was our second session together. The first hadn't gone much better. For a few moments I studied her slouched posture and the way she used her thumbnail to dig at the raw cuticles around her fingers, and I knew I was going to have to change the dynamic in the room if I was to get through to her. There was another seat beside Kate I usually reserved for couples therapy, but I got up and sat in it so I was roughly her mirror image, side by side.

I let that physical change settle in her. At first she seemed threatened, shifting away from me. I said nothing and waited until she lifted her head to look at me.

"What do you want?"

"To help if I can. To do that, I have to see the world the way you see it."

"So what, you sit next to me and expect to see the world the way I do?"

I ignored the caustic tone and said, "I sit next to you rather than comfort you, and maybe you give me a glimpse of your world."

Kate sat back, looked away from me, and said nothing for ten, then fifteen deep, ragged breaths.

"Yes, nine," she said at last. "Just before my tenth birthday."

"You knew him?"

"My Uncle Bert, my mom's sister's husband," she said. "I had to go live with them after my mom died."

"That's brutal. I'm sorry to hear that. You must have been terrified, betrayed by someone you trusted."

Kate looked at me and spoke bitterly. "It wasn't betrayal. It was a robbery, armed robbery. None of that slow grooming you hear about. Six months after I got there, my Aunt Meg went to visit friends for the weekend. Uncle Bert got drunk and came into my bedroom carrying a hunting knife and a bottle. He

24

THE DANGER THAT LURKS WITHIN

threatened me with the knife, told me he'd cut my throat if I ever said a thing. Then he pinned me facedown and—."

"You tell anyone?" I could see it in my head and felt sickened.

"Who would believe me? Uncle Bert just so happened to be the sheriff. Aunt Meg idolized him, the piece of shit."

"How long did the abuse go on?"

"Until I ran away. Sixteen."

"Your aunt never suspected?"

Kate shrugged and finally looked over at me. "When I was a little, little girl, I loved to sing with my mom in the church choir. My aunt was in a choir, too, and until Uncle Bert came into my room, singing with her was the only thing that made me happy. I could forget things, become part of something."

She was blinking, staring off now, and I saw

the muscles in her neck constrict.

"And after Uncle Bert?"

Kate cleared her throat, said in a soft rasp, "I never sang in tune again. Just couldn't hold a note for the life of me. Aunt Meg could never figure that one out."

"She never knew?"

"She was a good soul in her way. She didn't deserve to know."

"You weren't at fault, you know," I said. "You didn't cause the abuse."

Kate looked over at me angrily. "But I could have stopped it, Dr. Morris. I could have done what I wanted to do: snatch that buck knife off the nightstand when he was done with me and lying there all drowsy drunk. I could have sunk the knife in his chest, but I didn't. I tried, but just couldn't do it."

Kate broke down then and sobbed. "What

kind of coward was I?"

~ ~ ~

When Kate left my office twenty minutes later, I was wondering if my tactics had done any good. She'd opened up, and that was positive. But right after she called herself a coward, she clammed up tight again, said she hated thinking about those times. They made her cravings for the pipe and bottle more intense.

"See you at our next appointment?" I asked before she went out the basement door.

Kate hesitated, but then nodded. "Got no choice, right?"

"Judge wants it, but I hope you come to want it. This is a safe place, Kate, no judgments. Opinion only if you ask for it."

Her eyes roamed to my face, saw I was sincere. "Okay then, next time."

I'd no sooner shut the door than my cell phone buzzed in my office. I ran and grabbed it on the fourth buzz, seeing Sharon was calling for a second time.

"You already showered and off to work?" I said.

"I never made it home," she replied in a strained voice. "You haven't heard?"

"No. I've been in a session the past—"

"Someone put two bombs on the National Mall, E. J. Probes put me in command up on the Washington Monument where I could see everything. We got one neutralized before it exploded at 8:26. But I made a decision to send a bomb team to neutralize the second IED versus checking it first with the robot. When they were close, at 8:23, it went off. They're okay because of the mats and the suits, but it's a wonder they weren't killed."

"Jesus," I said. "How are you?"

"Shaken," she replied. "I haven't sent men in to get bombed before."

I winced. "I can't imagine, baby. What's Probes saying?"

"He has my back. Denton recommended the attempt. We had seven minutes, so I accepted her recommendation."

"How did you know you had seven minutes?"

"The bomber told me. He called my cell to warn me that an IED was supposed to go off at 8:26 a.m."

"Why you?"

"No idea. But he had my private number."

"No suspects?"

"We have a suspect in custody," she said, and told me about a man who'd waded into the reflecting pool before dismantling his pistol. "We want you to come in and talk to him ASAP."

"Uh, I'm suspended pending trial."

"Mahoney's taken the lead. He wants you there, and Probes will never know."

"Okay," I said uncertainly. "But I'm stacked with patients until two."

There was a pause before Sharon said, "Two bombs on the National Mall, E. J.?"

Even though she wasn't there with me, I held up my free hand in surrender.

"You're right. No argument. Where do you want me and when?"

"FBI building, ASAP. Bring me a change of clothes?"

"Absolutely," I replied, grabbing a pen to scribble notes on what she wanted. So much for my suspension.

# Chapter 4

I raced upstairs, got Sharon's clothes and basic toiletries in an overnight bag, and called a car through Uber that arrived in just a few minutes. I didn't want to drive my vehicle, so I left it home. The driver said that traffic was finally starting to move, as the police opened up the roads. I spent most of the ride calling patients to cancel appointments.

When I finished, I closed my eyes and shifted my thinking from the call of psychotherapy back to the craft of investigation, a craft that until five months before had consumed most of my adult life in six years with the Bureau's Behavioral Science Unit, and fourteen on and off with DC Metro's Major Cases team.

When I opened my eyes, it felt like I'd put on an old and familiar set of clothes and picked up tools that I could have used blindfolded. I have to admit, I felt full of renewed purpose when we pulled up in front of the J. Edgar Hoover Building.

Still in her running gear, Sharon was on the sidewalk waiting for me with special agent in charge Ned Mahogany, my old partner at the Bureau. As usual, he wore a dark Brooks Brothers suit, starched white shirt, and repp tie. Both he and Sharon looked big-time stressed. I climbed out, thanked the driver, and hugged and kissed Sharon before shaking Ned's hand.

Sharon took the overnight bag, checked it, and smiled at me, then Ned. "Is there somewhere I can shower and change inside?"

"Women's locker room," Ned told her. "I'll get you a pass."

"Perfect," she said, and we started up the steps to the front entrance.

"What do we know about the guy in the reflecting pool?" I asked.

Ned preferred to wait until we were inside and upstairs in a conference room, close to the interrogation room where they were holding retired Marine sergeant Timothy Cherry. Ned told us Cherry had done almost three full tours of duty in Iraq.

Two months shy of the end of that third tour, Cherry sustained a head injury due to an IED explosion in Helmand Province. The bomb killed two of Cherry's men, rattled his brain, and damaged his inner ears. He spent time in a US military hospital in Wiesbaden, Germany, before transferring to Bethesda Naval Hospital, where the neurological effects of the blast eased, but did not entirely disappear.

Cherry was granted a medical discharge nearly four years before he waded into the reflecting pool. He left Bethesda with bilateral hearing aids, determined to go to school on the GI bill.

"His behavior seems erratic at best," I said, reading from a VA doctor's notes taken on a walk-in visit a year after he left Bethesda. "Patient reports he has lost apartment, left school, can't sleep. Headaches, nausea are common."

"That's it. Cherry basically vanishes after that appointment," Mahogany said. "He goes underground for three years and surfaces to put bombs on the National Mall."

"If he's your bomber, Ned."

"He's the guy, E. J. Master gunnery sergeants like Cherry wear a bomb insignia on their left lapel, for Christ's sake. This guy may not have triggered the explosion, but he was involved. He ran from police, ignored their repeated orders, and was diverting attention from the bomb squad when that IED went off. And he hasn't said a word since we've had him in custody."

"Explosives residue on him?"

Mahogany grimaced. "No, but he could have worn gloves, and the techs say his dunk in the reflecting pool could have removed whatever traces there might have been."

"No lawyer?"

"Not yet, and he hasn't asked for one. He hasn't said anything, in fact."

"Mirandized?"

"Most definitely. Second they pulled him out of the water."

"Okay," I said, shutting the file. "Let me see if he'll talk to me."

~ ~ ~

As soon as Sharon returned after a shower

and a change of clothes, I went into the interr-ogation room alone. My first task was to build trust and see what Cherry might tell me of his own volition. Wearing an orange prison jump-suit, Cherry sat in a chair bolted to the floor, gazing intently at his grimy hands folded on the tabletop and the handcuffs that bound his wrists. A heavy leather belt encircled his wrist, with steel hoops attached to chains welded to the legs of the chair.

If he saw me enter, he ignored me. Not a flicker of reaction passed over his face. His entire being seemed focused on his hands and wrists, as if they held some great secret that calmed and fascinated him. He was, as Sharon had described him, six foot three and rail thin, with dull brown dreadlocks, a sparse beard over drawn skin, and dark bags under his eyes, which were still gazing, barely blinking. He stank of body odor and cheap booze.

"Mr. Cherry?" I said.

He didn't react.

"Gunny?"

Nothing. His eyes closed.

I was about to take the seat in front of him and shake the table so he'd open his eyes and at least acknowledge my presence, but then something dawned on me, and I eased to his side, studying him more closely.

I went around behind him and clapped my hands softly. Cherry didn't react. I clapped them loudly, and he didn't startle, but instead slightly cocked his head as if wondering if that sound was real.

"He's almost stone deaf," I said to the mirror. "That's why he wasn't responding to the officers' orders. And hate to say it, Ned, but it jeopardizes the Miranda."

Cherry opened his eyes and saw me in the mirror. He startled, squinted, and twisted around to look up at me. I held up my hands and smiled. He didn't smile back.

I went around the table, took another chair, and got out a legal pad and pen from my bag. I wrote on the pad:

"Master Gunnery Sergeant Cherry, my name is E. J. Morris. Can you hear with your hearing aids?"

Cherry brought his head close over the table when I spun it. He blinked, shrugged, squinted at me, and in a weird, hollow nasal voice said, "I don't know."

"Did you have them in when you went in the reflecting pool?" I wrote.

"Been two and a half years since I've had them. I think. Time goes by and—."

He stared off into the middle distance.

"What happened to them?"

"I got drunk, heard voices and that damn ringing in my head, and I don't know, I think I crushed them with a rock."

"Get rid of the voices and the ringing?"

He laughed. "Only if I keep drinking."

"Would it help if we got headphones and an amplifier for you?"

"I don't know. Why am I here? Is it that big a deal to protest in Washington? I've seen films of hundreds of peaceful protesters in that reflecting pool back in the sixties. Hell, they were in it in *Forest Gump*, right? Jenny was, anyway."

I smiled because he was right. Before I could scribble my response, a knock came at the door. An FBI tech entered with headphones, an amplifier, and a microphone. The tech put the headphones on Cherry and told me to speak.

Cherry shook his head at each hello. It wasn't until the amp was at 90 percent of capacity that he brightened.

"I heard it. Can it go louder?"

The tech said, "At a certain point it could further damage your ears."

Cherry snorted and said, "I already know what the silence is like."

The tech shrugged and turned the volume up again.

"Can you hear me?" I asked.

Both eyebrows rose, and he said, "Huh, yeah, I heard that in my right ear."

I set down my pen and leaned closer to the microphone the tech had set up on the table.

"Going in the water, dismantling your weapon, you did that as a protest?"

"Destroying my weapon was a protest. Beating swords into plowshares and baptizing

myself in the pool of forgiveness. It was sup-
osed to be a new beginning."

He said this with earnestness, conviction
even.

"You ran from the police."

"I ran from shapes chasing me," Cherry said.
"My eyesight sucks now, except right up close.
You can check."

"What about the bombs?" I asked. "The
IEDs?"

Cherry twitched at the word bombs, but then
appeared genuinely baffled.

"IEDs?" he said. "What IEDs?"

Chapter 5

Forty minutes later, I entered the observation booth overlooking the interrogation room where Cherry was still in restraints, sweating and moaning with his eyes closed. Ned Mahogany's arms were crossed.

"You believe him?" Mahogany asked.

"Most of it," I said. "You saw his hands there at the end. I'd say it would be impossible for him to build a bomb."

"Your wife saw him dismantle a Glock in under thirty seconds," Mahoney said.

"Once it's unloaded, a gun's no threat. Building a bomb, you can cross wires and blow yourself to kingdom come. Besides, you heard him, he's got an alibi."

"Sharon's checking it."

"Doc," Cherry moaned in the interrogation

room, "I need some help."

"I'd like to get him to a detox," I said.

"Not happening until we get a firm—"

The observation booth door opened. Sharon came in.

"The supervisor at the Central Union Mission vouches for him," she said. "Cherry slept there last night and left with the other men at 7:30. The super remembered because he tried to convince Cherry to stay for services, but Cherry said he had to go make a protest."

Mahogany said, "So what? He leaves the mission, picks up premade bombs, goes to the Mall, and—"

"The timing's wrong, Ned," Sharon insisted. "The bomber called me at 7:26 and again at 7:28, after he'd planted the bombs. The Mission supervisor said he was with Cherry between 7:20 and 7:30. During that time Cherry never asked for or used a phone, because he's, well, deaf. He left the mission on foot."

"The supervisor know about the gun?"

She nodded. "Cherry evidently turned it in whenever he came off the street to spend the night."

In the interrogation room, Cherry rocked in his chair.

"C'mon. Please, Doc. I got the sickness, man. The creepy-crawly sickness."

"He's not your bomber," I said.

"He could be a diversion," Mahogany said. "Part of the conspiracy. Besides, he had a loaded weapon in a national park, which is a federal offense. The park police will want him for that."

"The park police can get him for that once he's dry. They'll know exactly where he is, should they decide to press charges. Or you can send him to the federal holding facility in Alexandria, which is ill-equipped to handle someone with advanced delirium tremens, and you risk him dying before he can get clean."

The FBI agent squinted one eye at me.

"You should have been a lawyer, E. J."

"Just my professional opinion on a vet who has had a tough go of things."

Mahogany hesitated, but then said, "Take him to rehab."

"Thanks, Ned," I said, and shook his hand.

Mahogany shook Sharon's hand, too, saying, "Before I forget, Chief Stone, you impressed a lot of people this morning. Word's gotten around how cool you were under pressure."

She looked uncomfortable at the praise and gestured at me.

"You live long enough with this man and his grandmother, and you can handle anything thrown your way."

He laughed. "I can see that. Especially with his grandmother."

Sharon and I lingered in the hallway. She was returning to DC Metro headquarters to brief Chief Probes and to buy a second phone.

"I'm proud of you too," I said, and kissed her.

"Thanks. I just wish we'd been able to get the mats on that second bomb before— it will be interesting to see if it was a radio-controlled detonation."

"I'm sure Quantico's on it."

"See you at dinner?" she said as I went back to the interrogation room door. "Grandmom said she's creating a masterpiece."

"How could I miss that?"

Sharon blew me a kiss, turned, and walked away. I watched her go for a moment, more in love than ever. Then I turned the door handle and went inside, where retired Marine gunnery officer Tim Cherry continued to suffer for his country.

# Chapter 6

I got home around seven to find Sharon sitting on the front porch, looking as frazzled as I felt.

"Welcome home," she said, raising a mug. "Want a soda?"

I sat down beside her and said, "Sure, baby, but what I really want is you tonight."

"You're silly," she replied, passing me a glass of Pepsi.

I sipped it. "Nice and cold, just how I like it."

We sat in silence for several minutes, listening to the street and the rattle of kitchen utensils from inside.

"Tough day all around," Sharon said.

"Especially for you," I said, and reached out my hand.

She took it and smiled. "This is enough."

I smiled and said, "It is, isn't it?"

"All I could want besides that other thing you were talking about," she smirked.

"Don't invite me to a good time, little lady," I joked.

I focused on us. Not on the memories of how sick poor Cherry had gotten before I could get him admitted into the detox unit. How he'd refused to wear the hearing device or read my words after a while, retreating from the world and what it had done to him in the worst way he knew how.

"Dinner!" Grandmom Cheryl called.

Sharon squeezed my hand, and we went inside. My eighty-something grandmother was making magic at the stove when we entered the kitchen.

"Whatever it is, it smells great," I said, thinking there was a curry involved.

"It always smells great when Grandmom Cheryl's manning the stove," said Le'Shea, my oldest daughter, as she carried covered dishes from the counter to the table.

"Smells weird to me," said Shayana, my baby girl and the youngest, who was already sitting at the table, playing on her iPad. "Is it tofu? I hate tofu."

"As you've told me every day since the last time we had it," my grandmother said.

"Is it?"

"Not even close," she said, pushing her glasses up her nose on the way to the table. "No electronic devices at the dinner table, young lady."

Shayana groaned. "It's not a game, Grandmom. It's homework."

"And this is dinnertime," I said.

She sighed, closed the cover, and put the

tablet on a shelf behind her.

"Good," Cheryl said, smiling. "A little drum-roll please?"

Le'Shea started tapping her fingers against the tabletop. I joined in, and so did Sharon and Shayana.

"*Top Chef* judges," my grandmother said, "I give you fresh Alaskan halibut in a sauce of sweet onions, elephant garlic, Belgian blond beer, and dashes of cumin, cilantro, and just a bit of curry for the one who hates spicy food."

She smiled at me and popped off the lid. Sumptuous odors steamed out and swept my mind off my day. As we scooped jasmine rice and ladled the halibut onto our plates, I could tell Sharon had managed to put her day aside as well.

The halibut was delicious, and Cheryl's delicate sauce made it all the better. I had seconds, and so did everyone else. The fuller I got, how-ever, the more my thoughts drifted back to Cherry. Those thoughts must have shown on my face. My grandmother spoke up.

"Something not right with your meal, E. J.?"

"No, ma'am," I said. "I'd order that dish in a fancy restaurant."

"Then what? Your trial?"

I refused to give that a second thought.

"No, there was this veteran Sharon and I dealt with today. He suffered a head injury and lost most of his hearing in an explosion in Afghanistan. He lives in shelters and on the streets now."

Shayana said, "Dad, why does America treat its combat veterans so poorly?"

"We do not," Le'Shea said.

"Yes we do," Shayana replied again. "I read it on the internet."

"Don't take everything on the internet as gospel truth," Cheryl said.

"No," she insisted. "There's like a really high suicide rate when they come home."

"That's true," Sharon said.

"And a lot of them live through getting blown up, but they're never right again. And their families have to take care of them, and they don't know how," Shayana said. She was very smart to be nine years old.

"I've heard that too," my grandmother said.

"There's help for them, but not enough, given what they've been through," I said. "We brought the guy today to the VA hospital. Took a while, but they got him in detox to get clean. The problem is what's going to happen when he's discharged."

"He'll probably be homeless again," Shayana said.

"Unless I can figure out a way to help him."

My grandmother made a tsk noise.

"Don't you have enough on your plate already? Helping your attorneys prepare your defense? Seeing patients? Being a husband and father?"

Her tone surprised me. "Grandmom, you always taught us to help those in need. I'm only trying to do as I was taught."

"Long as you see to your own needs first. You can't do real good in the world if you don't take care of yourself."

~ ~ ~

"She's right," Sharon said later in our bathroom, after we'd cleaned the kitchen and seen the rest of the family to bed. "You can't be everything to everyone, E. J."

"I know that," I said. "I just—."

"What?"

"There's something about Cherry, how lost he is, how abandoned he's been, hearing nothing, seeing little. It just got to me, makes me want to do something."

"My hopeless idealist," Sharon said, hugging me. "I love you for it."

I hugged her back, kissed her, and said, "You're everything to me, you know."

"No, I don't," she smirked. "Why don't you prove just how much I mean to you?"

"Now you're speaking my kind of language," I replied, grabbing her butt.

"Let's go, big daddy," Sharon said, removing her shirt and pants as she made her way to our room. I followed behind her, trying to come out of my own clothes. Her body was very enticing.

We weren't even all the way in the room before Sharon was on her knees, with my hard-on in her mouth. I closed my eyes and enjoyed her warm mouth.

"That feels so good," I moaned.

Without missing a beat, Sharon stood up, turned around, pulled her panties to the side, and guided me inside her from behind. It felt like heaven. She knew how to make her muscles grip my rod and push the semen from it. We enjoyed each other's company until we fell asleep in each other's arms. That was what we both needed.

Chapter 7

At the mental health clinic of the Veterans Affairs Medical Center in northeast DC, in an outpatient room drenched in morning sun, a shaggy and shabbily dressed man in his early forties chortled bitterly.

"Thank you," he sneered in a falsetto voice. "Thank you for your service."

He shifted in his wheelchair and relaxed into a deeper, natural drawl that sounded like west Texas.

"I freaking hate that more than anything, you know? Can you hear me, folks? Can I get an aye?"

Around the circle, several of the other men and women, sitting in metal folding chairs, nodded, with a chorus of "aye." The group facilitator adjusted his glasses.

"Why would you hate someone showing you gratitude for your military service, Thomas?"

Thomas threw up his arms. His left hand and half the forearm were gone. Both of his legs were amputated above the knees.

"Gratitude for what, Jones?" Thomas said. "How do they know what I did before I lost two drumsticks and a wing? That's the hypocrisy. Most of the ones who wanna run up and tell you how much they appreciate your service, they never served."

"And that makes you angry?" Jones asked.

"Hell yeah it does. Many countries in the freaking world have some kind of mandatory public service. People who don't serve their country got no skin in the game as far as I'm concerned. They don't give a damn enough about our nation to defend it, or to improve it, or to lose limbs for it. They try to bury their guilt about their free ride in life by shaking my good hand and thanking me for my service."

He looked like he wanted to spit, but didn't.

"Why did you enlist?" Jones asked. "Patriotism?"

Thomas threw back his head to laugh. "Oh, God. Hell no."

Some of the others in the group looked at him stonily. The rest smiled or laughed with him.

"So why?" Jones said. Thomas hardened.

"I figured the army was a way out of East Jesus. A chance to get training, get the GI Bill, go to college. Instead I get shipped to pissed-off towelhead town. I mean, would anyone volunteer to go to the Middle East with a gun if the government offered college to someone who worked in schools, sweeping floors instead of getting shot? I think not. No freaking way."

"Damn straight," said Griffith, a big black

man with a prosthetic leg. "You're willing to whack 'em and stack 'em, they'll pay for a PhD. You wanna do good, they pay jack shit. You tell 'em, Thomas. Tell 'em like it is."

"If you don't, I will," said Mickey, who sat between Griffith and Thomas.

Jones glanced at the clock on the wall and said, "Not today, Mickey. We've gone over our time already."

Mickey shook his head angrily.

"You know they tried to do that to Donald Trump, shut off his microphone so folks wouldn't hear him before the election. Trump wouldn't let them, said he paid for the microphone. Well, I paid, Jones. We all paid. Every one of us has paid and paid, so you are not taking our microphone away."

The psychologist cocked his head.

"Afraid I have no choice, Mickey. There's

another group coming in ten minutes."

Mickey might have pushed his luck, seen if he could get a rise out of the shrink, something he enjoyed doing. But he felt satisfied that day. He decided to give Jones a break. Mickey waited until the psychologist left the room before rising from his chair.

"The powerful never want to hear the truth."

"You got that right, son," said Thomas, raising his remaining hand to high-five Mickey's.

"Scares them," said Keene, a scrawny guy in his twenties paralyzed and riding in a computerized wheelchair. "Just like Jack Nicholson said to Tom Cruise: 'They can't handle the truth.'"

"I'm still gonna speak truth to power," Mickey said. "Make them learn the lessons at gut level, know what I'm saying?"

"You know it," said Thomas. "Get an ice cream before you go home, Mick?"

Mickey wouldn't meet Thomas's gaze. "Stuff to take care of, old man. Next time?"

Thomas studied him. "Sure, Mick. You good?"

"Top notch."

They bumped fists. Mickey turned to leave.

"Give 'em hell out there, Mickey," Keene called after him.

Mickey looked back at the men in the wheelchairs and felt filled with purpose.

"Every day, soldiers," he said. "Every god-damned day."

~ ~ ~

Mickey left the VA through the north entrance and climbed aboard the D8 Metro bus bound for Union Station. Always sensitive to pity or suspicion, he was happy that not one rider looked his way as he showed his ride card to the driver and walked to an empty seat diagonally across from the rear exit. That was his favorite spot.

Mickey could see virtually everyone on the bus from that position. As he'd been taught a long time ago, to stay alive you made sure you could watch your six as well as your nine, twelve, and three.

In his mind, he heard a gruff voice say something.

"Understand your situation, soldier, and then deal with it as it is, not as you want it to be. If it's not as you want it to be, then fix it, goddammit. Identify the weakness, and be the change for the better."

"Damn straight, Hawks," Mickey thought. "Damn straight."

The doors sighed shut. The bus began to roll. Mickey liked buses. No one really noticed you on a bus, especially this bus. The inflicted and the wounded were a dime a dozen on the D8, the Hospital Center Line. Cancer patients. Alzheimer's patients. Head injuries. Amputees. They all rode it. He was just a bit player in the traveling freak show.

Which is why Mickey left the bus at K and Eighth and walked over to Christopher's Grooming Lounge on H. A burly barber with a lumberjack beard turned from the cash register and gave his client change. He saw Mickey and grinned.

"Hey, Mick! Where you been, brother?"

"Out and about, Fatz. You clean me up?"

"Shit, what's a Fatz for, right? You sit right here."

When Mickey got out of the chair twenty minutes later, his wispy beard was gone and his cheeks were fresh and straight razor smooth. His hair was six inches shorter, swept back, and sprayed in place.

"There," Fatz said. "You look somewhere between a hipster and a preppie."

"Right down the middle," Mickey said, turning his head. "I like it."

He gave Fatz a nice tip and promised to return sooner rather than later. The barber hugged him.

"I got your back. I'll always have your back."

"Thanks, Fatz."

"You're a good dude, remember that."

"I try," Mickey said, giving him a high five and leaving.

He walked the six blocks to the Capitol Self Storage facility at Third and N Streets and went inside to a small unit, where he unlocked and rolled up the door. Stepping inside, he pulled the door down and switched on the light. Six minutes later, Mickey emerged.

Gone were the dirty denim jeans, the canvas coat, and the ragged Nikes, replaced by khakis, a lightly used blue windbreaker sporting the embroidered logo of a golf academy in Scottsdale, Arizona, and a pair of virtually new ASICS cross-trainers. It was remarkable what you could find in a Goodwill store these days.

Mickey put on a wide-brim white baseball cap and a pair of cheap sunglasses. Around his waist, he wore a black fanny pack with a water bottle in a holder. Around his neck hung an old Nikon film camera with no film inside. "There," he thought as he locked the unit. "I could be any Joe Jackass come to town to see the sights."

Mickey left the storage facility and walked south, aware of the fanny pack, the water bottle, and the camera, and doing his best to contain his excitement. Be chill, brother. Stroll, man. What would Hawks say? Be who you're supposed to be. You're Joe Jackass on vacay. All the time in the world.

Fifteen minutes later, Mickey boarded the DC Circulator bus at Union Station with a slew of tourists. He stood in the aisle near the rear exit, holding the strap as the bus rolled down Louisiana Avenue. He got off at the third stop, Seventh Street, walked around the block, noted the increased police presence on the Mall, and returned to wait for the next bus to arrive.

He boarded it, found a spot as close as he could to the rear exit, and rode it until the eighth stop, the Martin Luther King Jr. Memorial. He got off. It was 11:00 a.m. Seventeen minutes later, Mickey reboarded the Circulator at the ninth stop, Lincoln Memorial.

Taking his usual position by the rear exit, Mickey felt lighter, freed, as if he'd left things in his past, on the verge of a brighter future. He waited to get off until the fourteenth stop, National Air and Space Museum. While tourists poured out the door after him, he dug in his pants pocket and came up with a burner phone.

He walked away from the knot of people trying to get into the museum and thumbed speed dial.

"Yes?" the woman said.

"Chief Stone?" Mickey said, trying to make his voice soft and low. "It's your worst nightmare again."

# Chapter 8

Sharon pulled down the sun visor flashers, hit the sirens, and told me to hold on. I braced my feet on the passenger side. She glanced in her side view and stomped on the gas. We squealed out of Fifth Street, ran the red light at Pennsylvania, and headed toward the Mall with Chief Stone calling the shots over a handheld radio.

"He says it's at the Korean War Memorial, but clear the MLK and Lincoln Memorial too," she said. "Close Ohio Drive and Independence Avenue Southwest. I want to know the second those five are clear. Am I clear?"

"Yes, Chief," the dispatcher said.

"Call IT," she said. "Find out if they got a trace on the call that just—"

Her cell phone started ringing. She glanced

down and said, "Forget it, they're calling me."

Cradling the radio mic, she snatched up her cell. "Chief Stone. Did you get it?"

Sharon listened and said, "How much damn time do they need?" A pause then. "You'd think in this day and age, it would be a hell of a lot less, but okay. If there's a next time, I'll try to keep him talking."

Hanging up and letting her phone plop in her lap, she let out a sigh of exasperation.

"A minute ten at a minimum to home in on an ongoing cell signal. He spoke to me for twenty-one seconds."

"They have no idea where he is?"

"Somewhere in DC, but they can't pinpoint the call. And even if they could, he has to be using a burner."

"You'd think," I said.

Six minutes later, Sharon threw the car in park near the Ash Woods on Independence

Avenue.

"You should stay here until you've got Mahogany at your side."

"Agreed," I said. "Be safe."

She kissed me on the lips.

"I'll let the pros take care of the dangerous stuff."

I watched her get out and walk toward the traffic barrier closing off the west end of the National Mall. She couldn't be seen bringing me into a Metro investigation while I was on suspension. Mahogany, however, could bring me in as a consultant. I left the car a few minutes later when he arrived with the FBI's bomb squad and a dog team of three.

The wind was out of the southeast, so Mahogany sent the dogs between the Lincoln Memorial and Korean War Veterans Memorial, a dramatic, triangular space with nineteen steel statues of larger-than-life soldiers on patrol,

THE DANGER THAT LURKS WITHIN

some emerging from a loose grove of trees and others in the open, walking across strips of granite and low-growing juniper.

The FBI dog handlers spread out and released the bomb sniffers. Muzzles up, panting for scent, they cast into the wind toward the statues. Back and forth they ran, coursing through the trees and the steel patrol soldiers. I stood beside Sharon, looking around to spot my favorite part of the memorial: these statues crouched around a campfire, set on a granite slab inscribed with "The Forgotten War."

"C'mon," Sharon said in a low voice. "Find it."

At the northeast end of the memorial, two of the dogs circled a low, dark wall that read "Freedom Is Not Free." They returned to their handlers waiting on the walkway. The third shepherd took a longer loop downward of the MLK Memorial before trotting back to his handler and the others.

"Rio and Ben are not picking up anything here," a handler said on the radio. "And Kelsey wasn't smelling anything at MLK. We can run the Lincoln if you want us to."

"Yes," Sharon said. "Better safe than sorry."

"The boy who cried wolf?" Mahogany said.

"An effective tactic," I said. "Gets us all worked up, calls us to action. He probably gets a kick out of—."

The bomb exploded behind us. We dove to the ground and covered our heads. Bits of gravel rained down on my back. When it stopped, I lifted my head to see a thin plume of charcoal-gray smoke rising to the right of a walkway that led toward King's Memorial.

"Jesus," Mahogany said, getting up and dusting his suit off. "How'd we miss that?"

"The dogs were just through there," Sharon said, rattled but fine.

The lead dog handler shook his head in bewilderment.

"If there was a bomb, they would have smelled it."

"Well, they didn't," Mahogany snapped before calling for a forensics team to gather the bomb debris for analysis.

We all put on blue hospital booties and moved toward the explosion site, everyone seeming jittery and uncertain. Yesterday he'd put two bombs on the National Mall. If the dogs didn't smell the first one, couldn't there be another?

No more than a foot across and five inches deep, the smoking crater was two feet off the pedestrian walkway, on the other side of a slack black chain fence. The bomb had been hidden under a low jumper, now charred and broken. A mangled, burnt metal casing lay on the ground several feet away.

"Looks like a camera body," Sharon said. "Or what used to be one."

That spooked me. How many tourists in DC carry a camera? It would never be noticed, at least not while the bomber was carrying it. He was smart. He was creative. But something about the explosion bothered me.

"It didn't do a lot of damage," I said. "I mean, it could have been bigger, made more of a statement."

"He wounded two agents yesterday," Sharon said.

"I'm not discounting that. It just seems like this should have been an escalation."

"Or at least two bombs," Mahogany said.

"Exactly."

Before Sharon could reply, one of the dog handlers yelled. He'd found something on the north side of the memorial.

"Is your dog on scent?" Mahogany shouted

74

as we hurried toward them.

"No," the handler said when we got close. "I saw it in that clear trash bag there, a black fanny pack."

Sharon triggered her radio and said, "Bring the bomb team up."

Within five minutes, FBI bomb squad commander Peggy Denton had arrived. We watched her iPad screen showing the Andros robot's camera feed and monitoring several electronic sensors. She shook her head.

"We're not picking up on a radio or cell phone. No timer either. We can X-ray it."

Mahogany nodded. Another tense three minutes passed while they moved a portable X-ray into position and looked inside the fanny pack. Aside from a water bottle and a shirt, there was an irregular rectangular item roughly three inches long, two inches wide, and two thick.

"Too wide for a Snickers bar," I said. "Brownie?"

"Too dense for either of them," Denton said. "Can't see any triggering device, no blasting caps, or booby trap lines."

"Your call," Mahogany said.

The commander put on her hooded visor, walked the thirty yards to the garbage, and retrieved the fanny pack. She unzipped it, reach-ed in, and pulled out the object, which was loosely wrapped in dull green wax paper.

"Shit," Denton said through her radio head-set. "I need a blast can here ASAP."

Another of the bomb squad agents hurried toward Denton with a heavy steel box.

"What's going on?" Sharon asked.

"It's C-4-type plastic explosive," Denton rad-ioed back as her partner opened the box's lid. She set the bomb material inside and screwed the lid shut. "Yugoslavian Semtex by the mark-ings on the wrapper."

"Why didn't the dogs smell it?" I asked. "Isn't there something added to plastic explosives so they can be detected?"

"They're called taggants," Denton said, taking off her hood and visor and coming back over. "I suspect this C-4 is old. Pre-1980, before taggants were required under international law."

Sharon shook her head. "Yesterday, the dogs smelled the bombs. Why make just one bomb out of it, but not four? And why leave the uncharged C-4 at all?"

"My guess is he left it as a warning," I said. "He used plastic explosives with taggant the first time, but that game's over. He's saying we can't sniff him out now. He's saying he can bomb us at will."

# Chapter 9

Tense days passed without a phone call from the bomber. Sharon was under pressure from Chief Probes. Mahogany was dealing with the FBI director. The only break came from the FBI crime lab confirming that the explosive used in the third bomb was pre-1980 Yugoslavian C-4, and that the triggering devices, all timers, were sophisticated. The work of an experienced hand.

I did what I could to help Mahogany between seeing patients, including Kate Williams, who showed up five minutes early for a mid-morning appointment. I took it as a good sign. But if I thought Kate was ready to grab hold of the life preserver, and I certainly hoped she was, I was mistaken.

"Let's talk about life after you ran away," I

said, then sitting down with my chair positioned at a non-confrontational angle.

"Let's not," Kate said. "None of that matters. We both know why we're here."

"Fair enough," I said, pausing to consider how best to proceed.

In situations like this, I would ordinarily ask a lot of questions about documents in her files, watching her body language for clues to her deeper story. Indicators of stress and tension, the inability to maintain eye contact, say, or the habitual flexing of a hand, are often sure signals of deeper troubles.

But I'd had difficulty reading Kate's body language, which shouted so loud of defeat that very little else was getting through. I decided to change things up.

"Okay, no questions about the past today. Let's talk about the future."

Kate sighed. "What future?"

"The future comes every second."

"With every shallow breath."

I read defiance and despair in her body language, but continued to talk.

"If none of this had happened to you, what would your future look like? Your ideal future, I mean?"

She didn't dismiss the question, but pondered it. She said, "I think I'd still be in, rising through the ranks."

"You liked the army."

"I loved the army."

"Why?"

"Until the end it was a good place for me. I do better with rules."

"Sergeant," I said, glancing at her file. "Two tours. Impressive."

"I was good. And then I wasn't."

"When you were good, where did you see yourself going in the army?"

I thought I'd gotten through a crack, but she shut it down. She said, "They discharged me, Dr. Morris. Dreaming about something that can never happen is not healthy."

She watched me like a chess player looking for an indication of my next move. Should I ask her to imagine a future for someone else? Or prompt her to take the conversation in a new direction? Before I could decide, Kate decided for me.

"Are you investigating the IEDs?" she asked. "On the Mall? I saw a news story the other night. Your wife was there, and I thought I saw you in the background."

"I was there, but I can't talk about it beyond what you've heard," I said. "Why?"

She stiffened. "Familiar ground, I guess."

I grasped some of the implication, but her body said there was more.

"Care to explain?"

"I know them," she finally said, struggling. "They're like rats. Digging in the dirt. Hoping you'll happen by."

"The bombers?"

Kate took on a far-off look. It seemed she was seeing terrible things, her face twitching with repressed emotion.

"Stinking sand rats," she said softly. "They only come out at night, Doc. That's a good thing to remember, the sand rats and the camel spiders only come out at night."

The alarm on my phone buzzed, and I almost swore because our hour was nearly up. I felt like we were just getting somewhere. By the time I silenced the alarm, Kate had come back from her dark place and seen my frustration.

"Don't worry about it, Doc," she said, smiling sadly as she stood. "You tried your best to crack the nut."

"You're not a nut."

She laughed sadly. "Oh yes I am, Dr. Morris."

# Chapter 10

Wiping at tears, Mickey left the VA Medical Center and ran to catch the D8 Metro bus heading south. He barely made it and wasn't surprised to find the bus virtually empty at this late hour. Breathing hard, Mickey went to his favorite seat, barely glancing at the only two other passengers, an elderly woman with a cane and a heavyset man wearing blue work coveralls.

As the bus sighed into motion, Mickey felt tired, more tired than he'd been in weeks, month's maybe. Rather than fight it all the way to Union Station, he pulled his baseball cap down over his eyes and drifted. Feeling the bus sway, hearing the rumble of the tires, he fell away to another time, in a place of war.

In his dreams, the sun was scorching.

Mickey had buried himself in a foxhole as the Taliban mortared an advanced outpost in the mountains of Helmand Province, Afghanistan. Each blast came closer and closer. Rock and dirt fell and pinged off his helmet, smacked the back of his Kevlar battle vest, made him cringe and wince, wondering at each noise if his time was finally up.

"Where the Christ is that number?" he heard a voice shout.

"Upper south hillside, two o'clock," another voice called back. "Three hundred vertical meters below the ridge."

"Can't find him," a gruffer voice yelled. "Gimme range!"

A third man yelled, "Sixteen hundred ninety-two meters."

"That ledge with the two bushes on the

right?"

"Affirmative!"

"I got it. Just has to show himself."

A fourth voice shouted, "Smoke him, Hawkes! Turn the sumbitch inside out!"

The mortar attack had slowed to a stop. Mickey got up, the debris falling off his uniform as he spat out dust and poked his head out of his foxhole. To his right about twenty yards, Hawkes was settled in behind the high-power scope of a .50-caliber Barrett sniper rifle.

Muscular and bare chested under his body armor, Hawkes had the stub of a cheap unlit cigar dangling from the corner of his lips.

"Take him out, Hawkes," Mickey yelled. "We got better places to be."

"We do not move until that good son of Allah shows his head," Hawkes shouted back, his head never leaving the scope.

"I wanna go home," Mickey said. "I want you to go home, too."

"We all wanna go home, kid," Hawkes said.

"I'm going surfing someday," Hawkes said. "Learn to ride big waves."

"North Shore, baby," Hawkes said as if it were a daydream of his too. "Banzai Pipeline. Sunset Beach and—. Hey, there you are, Mr. Haji. Couldn't stand the suspense, could you? Had to see just how close you came with those last three mortars to blowing the infields past paradise."

Hawkes flipped off the safety on the Barrett and said, "Sending boys."

Before anyone could reply, the .50-caliber rifle boomed and belched fire out the ported muzzle. In the shimmering heat Mickey swore he could see the contrail left by the bullet, ripping across space, 1,692 meters up the face of the mountain before it struck with deadly impact. The other men started cheering. Hawkes came off the rifle finally and looked over at Mickey with a big, shit-eating grin.

"Now we can go home, kid."

Mickey felt someone shaking him, and he startled awake.

"Union Station," the bus driver said. "End of the line."

"Sorry, sir, long day," Mickey yawned.

"For all of us. You got somewhere to be?" the driver asked.

"My mom's. It's not far," Mickey replied. He felt embarrassed answering him.

The driver stood aside for Mickey to go out the door. He went inside the bus terminal, following the signage toward the passenger trains and the Metro. Most of the shops inside Union station were closed and dark, though there were still a fair number of passengers waiting for Amtrak rides.

Mickey acted cold, pulled his hoodie up to cover his face from the security cameras, and went to short-term lockers, where he used a key to retrieve a greasy box of cold fried chicken from Popeye's. The last drumstick and wing tasted nice and spicy.

Mickey dropped the bones back in the box just as an overhead speaker blared: "Amtrak announces the Northeast Corridor Train to Boston, departing 10:10 on track 4. All aboard!"

With the cardboard box in his hand, he fished in his pocket for the ticket, fell in with the crowd, and moved toward the door to track 4. He showed his ticket to the conductor, who scanned it with disinterest, waved him through, and reached for the ticket of the passenger behind him.

Going with the knot of passengers, Mickey walked through a short tunnel that led out onto the platform. He passed the dining car and several others before spotting a trash can affixed to a post two cars back from the engines. He walked past it, never slowing as he dumped the greasy, fried chicken takeout box that held the bomb.

Then Mickey boarded the train and settled into a seat. His ticket said Baltimore, but he would get out at the first stop, New Carrollton, and catch the Metro back into the city, where he'd try to get a little sleep before making a call to Chief Stone.

# Chapter 11

Sharon's phone rang at five minutes to three in the morning. I groaned and turned over, seeing her silhouette sitting up in bed.

"Sharon Stone," she answered groggily.

Then she stiffened. Her free hand reached out and tapped me as she put the call on speaker.

"A city on edge," the voice purred. "A third bomb found. Fears of more to come."

The diction and tone of the bomber's voice were as Sharon had described it. I couldn't tell if it was a man or a woman talking.

"Are there more to come?"

"Every day until people start to feel it in their bones," the bomber said. "Until there's a shift in their mindset, so they understand what it feels like."

"What kind of shift? Feel like what?"

"Still don't get it, do you? Look in Union Station, Chief Stone. In a few hours it will be packed with commuters." The connection died.

"Shit," Sharon said. She threw back the covers and jumped out of bed, already making calls as she moved toward the closet.

I was up and tugging on clothes when central dispatch answered her call, and she started barking orders as she dressed.

"We have a credible bomb threat in Union Station," Sharon said. "Call Metro Transit Police. Clear Union Station and set up a perimeter outside. Get dogs and bomb squads there ASAP. Alert Chief Probes. Alert FBI SAC Mahogany. Alert Capitol Police. Alert the mayor and Homeland Security. I'll be there in nine minutes, tops."

She stabbed the bottom to end the call and

tugged on a blue sweatshirt emblazoned with Metro Police on the back. I was tying my shoes when she came out of the closet.

"What are you doing?"

"Going with you," I said. "Mahogany will be there soon enough."

Sharon hesitated, but then nodded. "You can drive."

Eight minutes later I slammed on the brakes and parked in front of the flashing blue lights of two Capitol Hill Police cruisers blocking Massachusetts Avenue and Second Street Northeast. Sharon jumped out, her badge up.

"I'm Metro Chief Stone."

"FBI bomb squad and a Metro's K-9 unit just crossed North Capitol Street, heading toward the station, Chief," one officer said.

"The station clear?"

"Affirmative," another officer said. "The last

of the cleaning crew just left."

Bree glanced at me, then looked back at the officers standing there.

"Dr. Morris is an FBI consultant on these bombings. He'll be coming in with me."

The officers stood aside. We hurried along deserted Mass Avenue toward the now-familiar vehicles of the FBI bomb squad and two Metro K-9 teams parked out in front of the station. Three men walked toward us wearing work-men's coveralls.

"You with the cleaning crew?" I asked, stopping.

The men nodded. Sharon said, "Catch up."

I asked them a few questions and found Sharon at the back of the FBI's Bomb Squad vehicle, where Peggy Denton was sitting up.

"Do we have a deadline?" Denton asked.

"It wasn't put that way," Sharon said. "Just

a suggestion to look in Union Station because at 6:00 a.m. the station will be packed with commuters."

"Awful big place to sweep in two hours and twenty minutes," Denton said, checking her watch.

"You can narrow it down," I said.

"How's that?" Sharon asked.

"Your bomber likes trash cans. Three of the four IEDs were in them. The cleaners I just spoke to said they were working from the front entrance north. They swept, vacuumed, and picked up trash bags in the main hall and on the first level of shops. Those garbage bags are in cleaning carts. Two are in the shopping hall and food court. One in the main hall. I'd take the dogs to those carts first and then sweep the second floor of shops and the Amtrak ticketing and the train platforms. Metro station after that."

The FBI bomb squad commander looked to Sharon.

"That work, Chief?"

"It does," she said. "Thank you, Dr. Morris."

"Anytime," I replied.

Ned Mahogany showed up, along with two FBI bomb-sniffing canines and the entire Metro Bomb Unit.

"We've got to stop meeting this way, Chief," Mahogany said, bleary-eyed and drinking a cup of Starbucks.

"Our secret's out," she said.

"He's escalating," I said. "The interval between attacks is getting shorter. Twenty-four hours between the first and the next two. And now fifteen hours since then?"

"Sounds right," Mahogany said, nodding. "How much time did he give us?"

"Two hours eighteen minutes," Sharon said. "Six a.m."

"If Dr. Morris is right and he hid it in a garbage can, we'll find it a lot sooner than that."

"Unless he's using Yugoslavian C-4 again," I said.

"Which is why we'll treat every garbage bag or can as if it's a live bomb."

The first dogs went inside at 3:39 a.m. We went in after the bomb squads entered, and stood in the dramatic vaulted main hall of the station, listening to the echoes of the dogs and their handlers. None of the K-9s reacted to the garbage carts the cleaners had abandoned. But Denton prudently had them turned over, dumping the trash bags, which she covered with bomb mats.

She couldn't do that to every remaining trash bag in the station. Instead, she told her agents to don their protective cowls. They would retrieve every public garbage bag left in the rest of the building and put them in piles to be matted.

They cleared the second floor of the shops first. I noticed and pointed to a *Washington Post* newspaper box. The headline read: "A City on Edge. Fears of More to Come."

"He was reading from the paper," Sharon said.

"Following his own exploits," I said. "Enjoying himself."

The dogs cleared the Amtrak hall.

"It has to be out on one of the platforms then," I told Sharon and Mahogany. "The cleaners said they almost always do them last."

Mahogany ordered the search personnel onto the platforms. We went through a short tunnel to platform 6 and watched as the German

THE DANGER THAT LURKS WITHIN

shepherds loped past dark trains, flanking platforms 1 and 2 to our far left, going from garbage receptacle to garbage receptacle, sniffing at the open doors to the coach cars. Sharon checked her watch.

"We'll find it," she said. "There's only so many places he could have—"

The tracks to both sides of platforms 4 and 5 were empty. There was nothing to block the brilliant flash of the bomb exploding in a trash can at platform 4's far north end, or the blast that boxed our ears and forced us to our knees. It was 4 a.m. on the dot.

# Chapter 12

Later that afternoon, I opened the door to Kate Williams, who actually greeted me before going into my basement office. She took a seat before I offered it.

"How are you?" I asked, moving my chair to a nonthreatening angle.

"Could be worse," she said.

"The headaches?"

"Come and go."

"Tell me about that day."

Kate stiffened. "That's the thing, Dr. Morris, I don't remember much of it. Getting your bell rung hard has a way of erasing things. You know?"

"Yes. What do you remember?"

She fidgeted. "Can we talk about something else today?"

I set my pen down. "Okay. What shall we talk about?"

"Your wife's a police chief?"

"Chief of detectives," I said.

"She's part of the IED investigation. I saw her on the news. You too."

"The FBI's brought me in as a consultant."

Kate sat forward in her chair. "What happened in Union Station this morning?"

"Beyond what's on the news, Kate, I really can't talk about it."

"But I can help you," she said eagerly. "If there's one thing I know, its IED bombers, Dr. Morris. How they think, how they act, what to look for, how to sniff them out. With or without dogs."

I tried not to look skeptical.

"It's what I did in Iraq," she said. "My team. We were assigned to guard supply convoys, but we were IED hunters, pure and simple."

Kate said her team, including a German shepherd named Brick House, rode in an RG-33 MMPV, a Medium Mine Protected Vehicle, which often led convoys into hostile territory. Her job demanded she sit topside in a .50-caliber machine gun turret, scanning the road ahead for signs of ambush or possible IED emplacements.

"What did you look for?" I said. I noted how much her demeanor had changed.

"Any significant disturbance in the road surface, to start," she said. "Any large boxes or cans on the shoulder of the road or in the brush. Any culverts ahead? Any bridges? Loose wires hanging to soil level from power poles. Any spotters on rooftops watching us? Men or women hurrying away from the road with red dirt all over their robes? Were they using cell phones? Were they using binoculars? If it was night, were we picking up anything in infrared images? It's a long list that gradually added up to gut instinct."

I studied her a long moment, wondering if it was possible she was involved. The bomber's voice had been soft, androgynous. But I saw no deceit in Kate's body language, nothing but openness and honesty.

"C'mon, Dr. Morris," she said. "I can help you."

"All right," I sighed. "I can't tell you every-thing. But, yes, an IED went off in Union Station early this morning. No one was hurt. The bomb caused minimal damage."

"Radio controlled?"

"Timer."

That seemed to surprise her, but she shrugged.

"He's not trying to hit a moving target, though, is he? What's the medium he's using? Fertilizer?"

I hesitated, but was intrigued by the line of questioning. "Plastic explosive."

"C-4. We saw that when they targeted bridges. Describe the placement?"

I told her that four of the five bombs had been found in trash cans, one buried beside a path between the Korean War and Martin Luther King Memorials.

"He's nervous," she said. "That's why he's using the trash cans. They're easy. Disguise it as something else, dump it, and walk on. How much power in the bombs?"

"You'd have to ask the guys at Quantico. They're analyzing what's left."

"But we're not talking significant damage here," she said. "There's no ball bearings or scr- ews wrapped around the C-4 to cause maximum mayhem."

"Not that I've heard."

She stared off. "That's when they're out for big blood. How's he warning you?"

We hadn't revealed that the bomber had been calling Sharon directly, so I said, "Warning us?"

Kate cocked her head.

"Every time a bomb's gone off, police and FBI have been on the scene, actively looking for a bomb. You had to have been warned."

"I can't talk specifics."

"Any Allahu Akbar, jihad stuff?"

"Not that I know of."

"That was another thing I was always tuned in to. I learned enough Arabic to look for jihadi phrases spray-painted near IEDs."

"Really?"

"Oh, all the time," she said.

"There's been nothing along those lines."

Kate chewed on that. "He giving you any motivation?"

"Changing people's mindset. Making them understand."

"You quoting him?"

"Yes."

She fell quiet for almost a minute and finally said, "He's no Middle Eastern terrorist, that's for sure."

"How do you know?" I asked. I agreed with her, but I still had to ask.

"Jihadists are in your face about why they're trying to blow you up," she said. "They'll take credit for it in the name of Allah or their chosen fanatic group. And the damage inflicted doesn't make sense to me. Rather than put five bombs out, why not use all that C-4 and make a real statement? Wrap it in bolts, washers, and nuts, and get it somewhere crowded, like the Boston Marathon bombers?"

That made sense, actually.

"So what's the mindset change he's after? What's he trying to make us understand?"

Kate bit at her lip.

"I don't know. But I have the feeling if you answer those questions, Dr. Morris, you'll find your bomber."

# Chapter 13

Heavy rain fell when Mickey left the VA hospital long after dark. As soon as he felt the drops lash his face, he let go of the emotion he'd been fighting to keep deep in his throat. He choked off two sobs but finally let tears flow. Who could tell he was crying in the rain anyway?

Certainly no one Mickey encountered between the hospital and the D8 bus stop. They were all bent over, hurrying for cover. He was alone on the bench when the Hospital Center bus pulled up. Mickey got on and was dismayed to find his favorite seat by the rear entrance taken, by a big Latino guy he recognized. Like almost everyone riding the Hospital Center Line from the north end, he'd been chewed up by war and was always pissed off.

Mickey nodded to the man as he passed and

took an empty spot two rows behind, intending to take his territory back as soon as the man left. But the bus was warm, and Mickey was as tired and dismayed as he'd ever been. What am I doing this for? Doesn't he understand? How can't he understand?

Tears welled up again. Mickey wiped his device frantically at them. He couldn't be seen crying here. Out in the rain was one thing, but not here. "Be a soldier, man," he thought as his eyes drifted shut. "Be a soldier."

Mickey dozed and dreamed of scenes he had imagined many times. He felt tires hit potholes, and he was no longer in the bus, but deep in the back of a US military transport truck taking him away from the firebase for good, heading straight to Kandahar, then Kabul, and home.

"You happy, kid?" Hawkes asked. "Going Stateside?"

Hawkes, the sniper, was sitting on the opposite bench, next to the tailgate, his Barrett rifle balanced between his legs, grinning like he'd just heard the best joke of all.

"Damn straight I'm happy, Hawkes," Mickey said.

"You don't look it."

"No?" Mickey said. "I'm just nervous, that's all. We're so close, Hawkes, I can taste it. No more crazy mofos in turbans lobbing mortars. Leave this shit behind for good. Go home and just— what are you going to do when you get home, Hawkes?"

Hawkes threw back his head and laughed, from deep in his belly.

"Kiss my wife and play with my little boy, Mickey."

"He'll be happy his daddy's home," Mickey said. "That's so—"

Automatic weapons opened up from high in the rocks flanking the road.

"Ambush!" Hawkes shouted. "Get down, kid! Everyone get—"

Hawkes vanished in a roar and a blast of fire that knocked Mickey cold. For what seemed an eternity, there was only darkness. Then neon light played on his eyelids, and someone shook his knee. Mickey started, and awoke to see the Latino guy with the attitude staring down at him.

"Union Station."

"Oh?" Mickey said. "Thanks."

He took his knapsack and left the bus, running to the terminal to get out of the rain. There were police officers all over the place, and dogs, and reporters. But not one of them paid Mickey any mind as he moved with the evening crowd toward the subway and train stations.

Avoiding the train or Metro platforms, Mickey instead cut through the main hall and out the front door. Four television news satellite vans were parked along Massachusetts Avenue, facing Union Station. When the klieg lights went on, he almost spun around and went back inside. Instead, he put up his hood and waited until two men much taller than him exited the station.

He fell in almost beside them, within their shadows, until they were a full block east of the television lights. Mickey left them and kept heading east past Stanton Park. He went to a brick-faced duplex row house on Lexington Place and used a key to get inside as quietly as he could.

Television light flickered from a room down the hallway. He could hear a woman singing with a backup band, really belting the song out, probably on one of those star search shows his mother loved, and he hoped the singing would be enough to cover his climb up the stairs.

But when he was almost at the top, the song ended. His mother yelled drunkenly.

"Mick, is that you?"

"Yes, Ma."

"There's leftover Popeye's in the fridge. You want it? And get me some ice."

"I'm tired, Ma," he said. "And I gotta be up early."

He didn't wait for a response, but dashed up the stairs, around the bannister, and into his room. He locked it and waited, listening for an indication of how drunk she was. A little plastered, and she'd shrug it off. A lot plastered, and she was likely to pound at his door and shriek curses at him. A minute passed, and then two.

Mickey tossed his knapsack on the floor, took off his raincoat, and dug beneath his mattress, coming up with a dog-eared paperback book he'd bought online for twenty-two dollars. He'd read *A Practical Guide to Improvised Bomb Making* at least eight times in the past few months, but he climbed on the bed and returned to the chapter on radio-controlled explosives.

Mickey read for an hour, studying the diagrams until he understood how to build the triggering mechanism and how best to trip it. Glancing at the clock on his dresser, he stifled a yawn. It was eleven o'clock. Opening a drawer in the nightstand, he retrieved one of six burner phones he'd bought online in a package deal from a dealer in Oklahoma. Then he called up the Voice Charger Plus App on his smartphone. Mickey started the burner, activated it with a pre-paid minute card, and dialed Chief Sharon Stone.

"They're not listening," he mumbled to himself as her phone rang. "Time to raise the volume."

# Chapter 14

Sharon was fighting to stay awake for the eleven o'clock news when her phone started buzzing and beeping in her purse. She struggled out of the easy chair in the front room at home and said, "Mute it."

I thumbed the mute button and said, "Speaker."

Nodding, Sharon got her phone and answered the call. The odd, soft, almost feminine voice spoke.

"Chief Stone?"

"Who are you? What's your name?"

After a long pause, he said, "Nick. Nick the Avenger."

Sharon glanced at me, pointed at her watch. I started timing. The FBI was monitoring and tracing all calls to her number. If she could keep him on the phone for just over a minute, they'd be able to locate him.

"Nick, what's it going to take to stop the bombings?" she asked.

That question was part of a plan we'd talked about in anticipation of his next call. We both believed we needed to draw the bomber out, get him talking about more than just his next target. After several moments, he spoke up.

"It's gonna take changes on Capitol Hill, Chief. Congress needs to get off its collective butt and start treating the people who fight their wars right. Until they quit kicking vets in the balls, it's time for everyone to feel what vets have suffered, what they still suffer. I'd clear the Washington Monument if I were you."

The line went dead.

"Son of a bitch," I said. "Forty-five seconds."

We grabbed raincoats and headed out into

the pouring rain. I drove. Sharon started making calls to close off the National Mall once again, and summon sniffer dogs and bomb squads. Ned Mahogany called me as I turned onto Independence Avenue.

"You hear it?" he asked.

"Yes. The trace?"

"Bomber's within five miles of Capitol Hill. Closest we got."

"Any luck with the surveillance tapes from Union Station?"

"I have four agents watching footage from the twenty-four hours preceding the explosion, working backward from the actual blast. So far, nothing."

"Quantico?"

"Initial reports on the first two bombs came back," Mahogany said. "The detonators are simple, the kind you might see on an IED in the

Middle East. But the explosive wasn't taggant-free C-4. That's why the dogs were able to locate them."

"So what was the explosive?"

"Black powder, like for muzzleloaders, but tricked out, made more powerful. A company out in Montana makes the stuff."

"So we can trace it?" Sharon asked.

"Not as easy as you think," Mahogany said. "There are no real restrictions on the stuff. You can order it from dozens of websites online, or buy it off the shelf at hunting and fishing stores. Surprising, but the company says they make and sell thousands of pounds of the stuff per year."

I thought out loud, "So he has knowledge of and access to a wide array of explosives. What kind of person would get that kind of knowledge and access? I mean to seek out and get the

C-4?"

"Money talks. You can buy nearly anything these days on the dark side of the internet," Mahogany said.

"Or he's someone with real training, a military sapper. Or ex."

"You mean like a Marine master gunnery sergeant?"

"Tim Cherry's in detox," I said. I started to see blue lights ahead of us, and cruisers blocking access to the Washington Monument.

"No, he's not," Mahogany said. "I had someone check. Cherry walked out four days ago, within hours of you dropping him."

## Chapter 15

Dawn came, and the rain had been torrential and relentless all night, hampering the search for the latest bomb. The dark, low-hanging clouds above the Washington Monument showed no sign of clearing. Sharon and I were in our car, taking a break from the rain, listening to the all-news radio station and drinking coffee. I was only half paying attention to the newscast, covering the latest bomb threat and the likely effect on commuter traffic.

I was still brooding over Tim Cherry. On the drive over to detox, he'd told me he was ready for change. He was tired of the streets, tired of living in a soundless world, and tired of being blasted all the time. Blasted. It was the exact word he'd used.

Had the deaf veteran been playing me the

entire time? I like to think of myself as a pretty shrewd judge of character and an excellent reader of body language. I'd honestly believed Cherry, and I'd gone to bat for him. The back door opened. Mahogany slid inside wearing an FBI rain slicker and ball cap. He pushed back the hood and spoke.

"It's a monsoon out there."

"Anything?" I said.

"We're positive the inner monument is clear. But this rain's killing us. Really messes with the dogs' noses."

"And he could have used the pre-1980 C-4 again."

"True. Could also be he's abandoned his penchant for garbage cans as bomb sites. We've checked every one in a mile radius."

"Are you hearing this?" Sharon asked.

We looked at her. She turned up the radio,

reporting on a veteran's appropriations bill stalked in the Senate. If the bill didn't make it to the president's desk before Friday, there would be slashing of funds for dozens of critical veteran's programs across the board.

"You think this has something to do with it?" Mahogany said.

"He talked about Congress not treating vets right," she said. "Maybe this is his motivation. He knows this bill has to pass in four days, so he's pushing."

"But he never mentioned that specifically?" Mahogany said.

"No," Sharon said. "He didn't."

"It's been seven hours since the call," I said. "Maybe there's no bomb this time. Maybe he's yanking our chain."

"What makes you think that?" Sharon said.

"It's a freebie. He gets us mobilized, on

edge, and the media worked into another frenzy, and he doesn't have to use an ounce of plastic explosives to do it."

"Well, he's got me on edge," Mahogany said. "Six cups of coffee and two hours of sleep in the last twenty-four is not the way to better mental health."

"No, and neither is thinking Cherry's our guy," I said, looking over the backseat.

Mahogany started to stiffen, but I held up my palm. "The bomber hears just fine. Unless Cherry's had a cochlear implant, he's not who's been calling Sharon. I read his medical files. There's no way he—"

Ned held up both hands.

"Agreed, E. J. He's not the caller. But he could be the caller's partner."

I couldn't dispute that possibility.

"Are you naming him a person of interest?"

"I'm supposed to have that conversation with the deputy director in about ten minutes," Mahogany said.

"You recommending it?" Sharon asked.

"I'd be remiss if I didn't."

I stifled a yawn and checked my watch.

"Patients?" Sharon asked.

"Just one. Eight o'clock."

"You could cancel."

"I'll power through and get some sleep afterward."

Before she could reply, her cell phone rang.

"Here we go," she said, snatching it up and answering it on speaker.

"I made a mistake," the soft, strange voice said. "Silly Avenger, I put that bomb in the Air and Space Museum."

# Chapter 16

At two minutes to eight, the bell at our basement door rang, and I snapped awake from dozing in my office. After leaving Sharon and Ned on the Mall in front of the National Air and Space Museum, I'd come straight home and shut my eyes.

"Coming!" I called, then went in the bathroom to splash cold water in my face.

I opened the door. The rain had let up, and Kate Williams was beaming at me.

"Were you at the scenes this morning?" she asked, sounding breathless and excited.

"All night," I said, following her toward my office.

"Oh? Well, I'm glad you didn't cancel, Dr. Morris. I think I found something, something about the bomber."

I closed my office door, feeling a headache coming on.

"You know Kate, the FBI, Metro, Park Police, and Capitol Hill Police are working this pretty hard." Her expression turned stony.

"And you don't think I could come up with something the professionals couldn't."

"I didn't say that."

"You implied it."

I rubbed at my temples and took a seat.

"If I did, I apologize to you. I haven't had much sleep. I've just found over the years that when amateurs get involved with cases as big as this one, they can find themselves working at odds with the authorities, and some get charged with obstruction."

Kate crossed her arms. "I am not an amateur. I hunted bombs and bombers on a daily basis for more than three years, Dr. Morris. I've been in on explosive charges as many times as or more than anyone on your bomb squads."

"I get it, but with bombs and bombers, there are protocols determined by people with bigger brains than mine, who—"

I was surprised when she suddenly burst into tears.

"You don't get it do you? I have to do this, Dr. Morris. I have to help. You asked me about that day I got hit? I missed something. I turned the wrong way and missed something, and four IEDs went off at once. When I woke up, three of my people were dead. Brick House was dead too. I lived, and good friends and the sweetest dog I've ever known died, Dr. Morris. So do you want to hear what I have to say, or not?"

"I'm sorry," I said, holding out my hands. "Of course. What have you got?"

Kate dug in her raincoat pocket and came up

with a tourist map of Washington DC, which she unfolded and laid on the rug between us. Kneeling, she showed me where she'd marked and highlighted the bomb sites.

"Mall in front of the National Sculpture Museum," she said. "Constitution Gardens Pond. Korean War Memorial. Union Station. Washington Monument."

"False alarm there," I said.

"It doesn't matter," she said before stabbing her finger at the map. "Air and Space Museum."

"I'm predicting a false alarm there as well."

"Like I said, it doesn't matter if bombs were there or not."

Ignoring the soft pounding at the back of my skull, I said, "Okay."

"What do they have in common?"

"They're all in and around the Mall?"

Reaching into her raincoat pocket again, she

came up with a Metro transit map.

"They're also all on this city bus route that started up in 2018," she said. "The DC Circulator. It starts at Union Station and goes all around the monuments with stops that line up with the bombing sites."

Instantly alert, I sat forward and studied the transit map.

"See?" Kate said. "I'm telling you, Dr. Morris. Your bomber rides that bus."

# Chapter 17

Two days passed without a call from the bomber. The deadline for the veteran's appropriations bill loomed, with no sign that the IEDs on the National Mall were having an effect on Congressional gridlock. Senators on both sides of the aisle continued to maintain their support of veterans yet fight every effort to get the spending bill on the president's desk.

I'd told Mahogany and Sharon about Kate Williams's theory that the bomber was using the DC Circulator, and they'd given it enough credence to have agents and detectives interview the route's drivers. None of the drivers had noticed anything out of the ordinary. Then again, it was cherry blossom season. Even with the bombings and the threats, the Circulator continued to be packed with tourists.

In a meeting at FBI headquarters that Wednesday morning, Mahogany typed on his laptop.

"My agent missed it the first two times through, but he may have forced something in the security video shot inside Union Station the night before the explosion. Look for the garbage can at center right."

The screen at the far end of the conference room lit and showed forty, maybe fifty people walking on platform 4 alongside an Amtrak train. The garbage can was blocked from view as passengers moved toward the last few cars.

"Any one of them could have planted it," Sharon said when the footage stopped with the platform clear. "And there had to be other trains that used that platform earlier."

"True, but watch the sequence again," Mahogany said.

He backed the video up twenty-five seconds.

"Look for the one in the black hoodie carrying the book bag."

Sharon and I studied the crowd, seeing several weary men and women in business suits, K Street types working late, carrying briefcases and trudging along. Behind them walked a person of medium build, likely a male, wearing a black hoodie that was up, casting the face in shadows. His shoulders were hunched forward, his head down and turned, as if he knew the position of the cameras.

"Watch for the moment John Doe and the people in front and behind him go by the trash receptacle," Mahogany said.

It took them no more than two seconds to go by the trash can, and I didn't catch what Mahogany was talking about. But Sharon did.

"We can't see his left arm, but his shoulder moved, and there was a flash of yellow near the mouth of the trash can."

"Exactly," Mahogany said. He backed it up, froze the tape on that moment, and magnified the screen so we could see exactly what was being junked.

"Popeye's chicken?" I said.

"A take-out box for a five-piece dinner assortment," Mahogany said.

"Okay?" Sharon replied.

"Now look at this footage from eleven minutes earlier."

The screen jumped and showed the same person, wearing jeans and black shoes, hoodie up, face blocked from view, standing near some lockers and a trash can. He was eating a drumstick from a yellow Popeye's box. He finished it, put the bone in the box, and then walked away when the Acela to Boston was called for boarding.

"That's our bomber," I said. "He could have trashed the box right there."

"Exactly," Mahogany said. "Why wait?"

Sharon's phone and my phone buzzed almost simultaneously. I looked down at the text and jumped to my feet. Sharon did the same.

"What's going on?" Mahogany said.

"Someone called in a bomb threat to Le'Shea's high school," I said.

Ignoring the fact that I was suspended from the force, I followed Sharon to her squad car. We raced north through the city, sirens and lights flashing, to Benjamin Banneker Academic High School. We stopped at a patrol car blocking access to Sherman Avenue and Euclid Street.

It was ten in the morning, almost hot, and though they were well removed from school property, the kids gathered on sidewalks and lawns looked anxious.

"Everyone's out?" Sharon asked the principal, Sheila Jones, a woman we both liked and respected.

"They know the drill. This has happened before, Chief Stone," Jones nodded.

"Bomb scares?" I asked.

"It's usually a student or a friend of a student who's behind on their studying before a big test. At least that's my theory, because nothing ever comes of it."

"Or hasn't yet," Sharon said. I scanned the crowd of students for Le'Shea.

"Were there big tests coming up?" I said.

Jones frowned. "Not school-wide tests. They just finished midterms."

"Dad?"

I turned to find Le'Shea had come up behind us. Looking very upset, she threw her arms around me and hugged tight.

"You okay, baby?"

She looked at me, shaking her head, on the verge of tears. "Don't you know?"

"Know what?"

"The threat, Dad. It was called in to me."

# Chapter 18

Less than three miles to the south, Kate Williams sat in the left-side window seat three rows behind the driver of the DC Circulator bus, where she could study everyone who came aboard and yet not attract attention.

Kate herself had boarded at 6:30 a.m. Four hours of riding, on top of fourteen hours she'd spent on the bus line the day before, and twelve hours the day before that.

"I don't care what I feel like, or how sore my butt gets," she mumbled to herself, fighting off a yawn as the bus pulled over near the Vietnam Memorial. "Whatever it takes."

She got off at the Vietnam Memorial to stretch her legs, use the public restrooms, and buy a warm pretzel and a diet soda from one of the vendors along Constitution Avenue. Another

Circulator bus would come along soon, and she could resume her vigil.

"He rides this bus line," Kate thought again, feeling irritated. "I'm sure of it."

Dr. Morris had been interested enough to pass her suspicion along to the FBI and to his wife, but they'd decided against putting surveillance on the routes, relying on the recall of the bus drivers. She couldn't understand it.

"That's just moronic. What do bus drivers know about bombers?"

Eating her pretzel slowly, Kate scanned the steady stream of tourists heading toward the Vietnam Memorial. There seemed even fewer tourists out today than yesterday, when crowds were noticeably lighter than the day before. In the dwindling pool, she felt certain she'd spot the bomber at some point.

And she was confident a solid look would be

enough. Kate had the ability to remember faces and recall them later, as in years later, even when the person had aged. Scientists called people with Kate's gift "super recognizers." The trait had helped her in Iraq. Unless the person was wearing a veil or a turban that obscured their features, she remembered their faces—especially in places where IEDs were actively in use.

Kate believed the skill would help her here. She kept combing the crowd, especially the people coming off the Circulator buses, recording faces, looking for twitches in their cheeks, or a slight hesitation when they passed the pair of police officers flanking the entrance to the walkway and the memorial.

Noticing that the hand of a woman her age shook visibly when she raised a coffee cup passing the cops, Kate focused on her face.

Click. She noted the excited expression of a young teenage boy coming off the next bus, in a blue school windbreaker with a hood. He was laughing and staring at his phone, watching a video, no doubt. Pass.

Then she studied a red-faced, angry-looking old guy who got off, wearing a red felt vest festooned with military pins. Click. A tall, lanky, bearded guy in filthy army camo fatigues shuffled slowly toward her, heading west. He pushed a shopping cart filled with plastic bags and God only knew what else. Click.

As he came closer she saw his skin was smeared with grime. His dark hair was matted, and he had an odd wildness in his eyes, as if he were on drugs. Click. Click.

A cop on Constitution Avenue lit up his siren for one whoop. It startled Kate, but the homeless vet seemed not to notice at all as if he were one of those fanatics she knew all too well, the ones getting ready to kill or be killed. Click. Click. Click.

There was something about him, something about that grocery cart. Maybe she'd been wrong. Maybe the bomber didn't use the bus line. Maybe he was just some homeless, off-the-radar guy, pushing a cart around filled with explosives.

Kate started to follow him, staying four or five people back. The tourists kept a wide berth as he moved resolutely west, and she understood why. He stunk bad. "This could be my guy," she thought. Her smartphone vibrated in her pocket. Kate dug it out, still trailing the homeless man.

She glanced at the screen, seeing a notify-cation from Twitter. She'd set an alert for the posts from a local news reporter to make sure she'd see any update on the DC bombings.

The tweet linked to a *Washington Post* story, "DC High School Under Bomb Threat."

She asked, "The bomber again? Leaving the Mall?"

Kate slowed her stride and clicked on the link, glancing at the homeless man's progress before reading the breaking story. Benjamin Banneker High had been evacuated on a bomb threat twenty minutes earlier, she read. K-9 and bomb squads were on the scene. The bomber's call had gone to an unidentified student, who had notified school administrators and the police.

Banneker? Something about that nagged at her. She used Google Maps to calculate the distance from her location to the school. It was 2.6 miles, give or take. Kate clocked the homeless vet, still shuffling west. The school wasn't that far, but there was no way that guy was walking 2.6 miles in twenty minutes, or even an hour or two. And she couldn't believe he owned a phone, much less used one to call in a threat.

Kate stopped, feeling doubt in her instincts for the first time, watching until she couldn't see him anymore. She turned away and headed back toward the Circulator bus stop. She knew the high school was far off the National Monuments bus route.

"Maybe I'm wrong," she mumbled to herself, the purposeful spirit of the last two days sinking. "Maybe I'm the moron."

~ ~ ~

By three that afternoon, Benjamin Banneker had been cleared for after-hours activities. Like the threats to the Washington Monument and the Air and Space Museum, it appeared to be a false alarm. Leah described the caller as a guy with a deep, hoarse voice, who told her there was a bomb in the school and hung up.

Sharon and I debated the likelihood that the incident was linked to the National Mall bombings. Did we have a copycat at play? Banneker was not far from the Mall, maybe two and a half miles, but what was the message here? There was symbolism in disrupting access to the national monuments to avenge the wrongs done to veterans. It sent a clear, if misguided, message. How did our daughter's charter high school fit into that?

Disturbingly, the caller had Le'Shea's phone number, and the Mall bomber had Sharon's. We theorized that someone might have hacked into one or both of their phones, or downloaded their contact info from someone else. But when? And how?

These questions were still whirling around in

my head early that evening when I boarded the DC Circulator Bus near the World War II Memorial. When I looked in and saw the person sitting three rows behind the driver, I smiled. I paid the fate and took a seat next to Kate Williams, who stared straight ahead, looking like a poker player who'd been up too long.

"Thought surveillance wasn't worth it," she said.

"I didn't say that. People over my pay grade make that decision."

She didn't reply.

"You still think he rides this bus?"

"I'm here, aren't I?"

"How long have you been looking for him?"

Kate shrugged. "I don't know, forty, forty-one hours total."

I gave her an appraising glance. "In the past four days?"

"Whatever it takes, Doc."

We pulled up to the Washington Monument stop, and I watched Kate studying each person who came on the bus. When they'd all paid their fares and taken their seats, I spoke.

"What exactly are you looking for?"

"Their faces."

As we drove on, making a few stops over the next ten or fifteen minutes, Kate explained her innate skill. I'd heard of super recognizing and its opposite; some people could remember every face they'd ever seen, and others could not remember even familiar faces.

"Any interesting faces so far?" I asked as we left the US Capitol stop.

"They're all interesting."

"No duplicates?"

"A few times, but they're usually tourists coming on and off, and I'll remember them from a few hours before."

"How about standouts? Someone who really hit you between the eyes?"

"You mean, like my spider sense?"

"Sure."

Kate tilted her head, thinking.

"There was one, earlier today. But he wasn't on the bus. He was this homeless guy in army fatigues, big crazy beard, pushing this grocery cart piled with his stuff in plastic bags, and he looked so . . . vacant . . . so . . . I don't know. More than drugs. Like he was unplugged. I mean, a cop lit up his siren maybe fifty feet from him, and the guy didn't startle, didn't even flinch. For some reason, seeing that, every alarm in my head started ringing."

Every alarm in my head started ringing as well. I asked her to describe the homeless guy in detail. As we pulled into the bus depot at

Union Station, the end and beginning of the Circulator line, there was little doubt in my mind she was talking about Tim Cherry, the deaf vet who'd dismantled his Glock and submerged himself in the reflecting pool the day of the first bombing.

I didn't tell that to Kate, though. She said, "I've had enough for today. Think I'll catch a cab, head home from here."

"I'll get off here, too," I said, glancing at my watch. "A walk over the hill will do me some good."

Night had fallen during our ride. As we exited, a bus lumbered and sighed into the parking bay beside ours. The digital sign above the windshield blinked from D8—Hospital Center Line Southbound to Union Station.

"Good night, Dr. Morris," Kate said, shaking my hand. "I appreciate you thinking enough of my theory to check it out."

"A good idea is a good idea," I said, and happened to glance over her shoulder at the sign on the other bus, now emptying of rides. The direction had changed.

D8—Hospital Center Line Northbound, it blinked. Veterans Affairs Medical Center.

# Chapter 19

I wished Kate Williams a good night and watched her walk off. Then I climbed on the empty Hospital Line bus. The driver, who looked to be in his fifties, was drinking coffee from a thermos, an egg salad sandwich in cellophane in his lap. I noted his name, Gordon Jacobs, posted at the front of the bus. I identified myself as a consultant with the FBI, which he met with skepticism.

"And how do I know you're not messing with me?"

"I can give you the private phone number of the special agent in charge of the bombing investigation," I said. "His name's Ned Mahogany."

He shifted in his seat.

"I gotta be out of here in ten minutes. What

do you want?"

He turned out to be a nice guy. I asked about the people who rode the Hospital Center Line, and Jacobs said that during the day, in addition to the folks who lived along the route, you had sick people.

"Lots of them. Four big hospitals and a bunch of clinics on the line. That's why we got the wheelchair lift."

"Veterans?"

"Lots of them too. You know, lost their arms and legs. Or their eyes. Or worse, their— you know."

I got it. "How do you know that?"

"It's in everything about them, man," Jacobs said quietly. "They look so damn humiliated. Can't even pick their heads up. I feel so bad for those boys. And for the families, you know?"

"Lot of family members with them? The

patients, I mean."

"You know, with all the non-vets stopping at Children's or Washington Hospital and the National Rehab, half and half maybe. Some relatives are very loyal, and you recognize them. There's this one couple. He's in a wheelchair, and there's his sister right behind him every time they get on."

"So you got regulars?"

"Oh yeah," he said, taking a bite of the sandwich. "But they'll come and go. Very few stick around forever."

"Sure," I said. "You must hear things driving."

Jacobs swallowed before letting out a laugh.

"You wouldn't believe the things I've heard! What people say out loud in public, as if I wasn't even there. Make my mother blush."

"Ever hear any of the vets talking trash

about the government? Congress?"

His laugh this time sounded bitter. "All the damn time." He thought about that. "Well, they all do it. One snafu after another for the vets, you know. But there's this one guy who rides once or twice a week. He's got nothing but piss and venom to say about the whole lot of them at the VA and up on the Hill. How the Capitol should explode."

"He said that?"

"Yup, a week, maybe two ago. You bet."

"You got a name for him?"

Jacob pursed his lips, shook his head. "Not that I've ever heard."

"But you'd recognize him?"

"He stands out. Half his face got chewed up by an IED."

~ ~ ~

At 8:30 the next morning, Sharon and I were

at the front entrance of Veterans Affairs Medical Center. We went straight to the plastic surgery unit, asked for the chief resident, and soon found ourselves in the office of Dr. Richard Smith.

We explained who we were looking for. Smith began to explain the various reasons he couldn't help us, starting with doctor-patient privilege, not to mention the HIPAA laws.

"We have reason to believe he may be involved in the Mall bombings," Sharon interrupted. "We have reason to believe that he is doing this because of Congressional gridlock over the veteran's bill."

Smith frowned.

"If it's the man I'm thinking of, this is surprising. Stunning even. As for the gridlock, I condemn the bomber's tactics, obviously, but the fact is that most of the programs in this building will shut down if that bill doesn't cross the president's desk. He's not the only one with a grudge."

"And if his next bomb kills someone?" I said. "Isn't that against the Hippocratic Oath—first do no harm? We need your help."

"We'll find him sooner or later. If we find him sooner, we save lives."

The doctor thought for a beat, then said, "You didn't hear this from me."

"Of course not."

"I think the angry vet you're talking about is named Juan Nico Vincente."

Smith would not give us Vincente's address or any of his records without a subpoena, but he did say the veteran had survived a brutal IED explosion in Afghanistan and suffered from head trauma and post-traumatic stress.

"He come to see you often?" I asked.

"Far as my area is concerned, there's nothing more I can do for him. But he's in the building a few times a week, sees a whole menu of docs and therapists. Hang out in the lobby long enough, and I'm sure he'll walk by."

As we left the hospital, Sharon was already running Vincente's name through a law enforcement database. He was on full disability from the army and had several priors for drunk and disorderly, incidents occurring at bars around his government-subsidized apartment in northeast DC. We drove there, to a brick building off Kansas Avenue. Mahogany met us out front.

"You really think this is our guy?" Mahogany said.

"By all accounts, he's a very angry dude," Sharon said. "And he'll probably get hurt big time if the veteran's bill doesn't go through."

Vincente lived on the fifth floor at the rear of the building. Most apartment complexes clear out during the day, with people at work and children at school. But with many residents of this building on disability, we heard televisions and radios blaring and people talking and laughing.

But not behind Vincente's front door. Before we could knock, we heard him ranting: "Senator Pussy, you evil, lying, son of a bitch! You never served! I swear I will come up there, get my rotted face in yours, and show you what this is all about! Right before I stick my KA-BAR up your asshole."

# Chapter 20

We all glanced at one another.

"That works," Mahogany said, and knocked at the door.

"Go away," Vincente yelled. "Whoever the hell you are, go away."

"FBI, Mr. Vincente," Mahogany said. "Open up."

Before we heard footsteps inside Vincente's place, a few doors to our left and right opened, revealing residents peeking out at us. Vincente's door creaked as if he'd put both hands on it. The light filtering through his peephole darkened. Mahogany had his ID and badge up. So did Sharon.

"What's this all about?" Vincente asked.

"Open or we break the door down, Mr. Vincente."

"Jesus," Vincente slurred.

Deadbolts threw back. The door opened, and a barefoot, narrow-shouldered man in gray sweatpants and a Washington Nationals jersey peered out at us with bloodshot eyes. It was hard not to look away. From scalp to jawline, the entire left side of his head was badly disfigured. The scarring on his face was ridged and webbed, as if the skin of many ducks feet had been sewn over his flesh.

He seemed amused at our reactions.

"Can we come in, sir?" Mahogany asked.

"Sir?" Vincente said, and laughed bitterly, before throwing the door wide. "Sure. Why not? Come in. See how the Phantom of the Opera really lives."

We entered a pack rat's nest of books, mag-azines, newspapers, and vinyl records. Stuff was almost everywhere. On shelves and tables. On the floor along the bare walls. And stacked below a muted television screen, showing C-SPAN and the live feed from the US Senate floor.

Streaming across the bottom of the screen it said, "Debate over relief act, and Senate bill 1982, veteran's appropriations."

I noticed an open bottle of vodka and a glass pitcher of tomato juice on a crowded coffee table. The ashtray next to them reeked of marijuana. Vincente threw up his hands.

"You've basically seen it all. My bedroom's off-limits."

"Nothing's off-limits if I think you have something to do with the bombings on the National Mall, Mr. Vincente," Mahogany said.

"The what—?" He threw back his head and laughed again, louder and more caustic. "You think I got something to do with that? Oh, that'll seal it. Just put the dog-shit icing on the crap cake of my life, why don't you?"

Sharon gestured at the screen.

"You're following this debate pretty close."

"Wouldn't you if your income depended on it?" he said darkly. He reached for a half-full Bloody Mary in a highball glass. "I decided to treat the floor debate like it was draft night for fantasy football leaguers. Right? Have a few Bloody M's, scream at the screen, 'Senator Pussy,' or whatever. No federal offense in that, is there, Agent Mahogany?"

"You ride the Hospital Center bus, Mr. Vincente?" I said.

"All the time."

"How about the Circulator? The Monument bus?"

He shook his head.

"They won't let someone like me ride the

Circulator. Upsets the tourists. Don't believe me? I'll let you check my bus pass. It'll show you. I only use the D8."

"That would help," Mahogany said.

Vincente sighed. "Hope you got time. Gotta find my wallet in this mess."

"We got all day," Sharon said.

He sighed again and started ambling around, looking wobbly on his feet.

"We hear you get angry on the bus," Sharon said, putting her hand on her service weapon.

Vincente took a sip of his Bloody Mary and raised it to us with his back turned, still searching. He squinted down and moved aside some record albums.

"From time to time, Chief Stone, I speak my mind forcefully. Last time I looked, that's still guaranteed under the Constitution I was maimed for."

Mahogany also put his hand on his weapon.

"Even under the First Amendment, the FBI takes seriously any threat to bomb Congress."

Vincente chuckled, stood unsteadily, and turned. Both Sharon and Mahogany tensed, but he was showing us a wallet in one hand and a Metro bus pass in the other.

"It was a turn of phrase," he said, holding out the pass to Mahogany. "I've had this for three years. It'll show I have never once been on the Circulator. And look at my record. I was a camp cook, ran the mess, not the armory in Kandahar. I honestly don't know the first thing about bombs. Other than they hurt like hell and they screw you up for life."

# Chapter 21

It was abnormally chilly and drizzling when Mickey climbed aboard the Hospital Center bus, taking his favorite seat at the window toward the back. He readjusted his windbreaker and the hoodie and vest beneath it so that he could breathe easier.

He wanted to explode. All day, the Senators talked and talked and did jack shit. That one over-educated idiot from Texas talked for hours and said nothing.

"How can that be? That's gotta change. It's gonna change. And I'm gonna be the one to change it. They're gonna talk all night, right? I got all night, don't I?"

Mickey had watched the floor debate from the first gavel, growing increasingly angry. As his bus left Union Station and headed north, he felt woozy and suddenly exhausted. Being angry for hours and days on end was draining. Knowing he'd need his energy, he closed his eyes and drifted off.

In Mickey's dreams, an elevator door opened, revealing a scary, antiseptic hallway inside Landstuhl Regional Medical Center next to the US airbase at Ramstein, Germany. Men were moaning. Other men were crying. Outside a room, a priest was bent over in prayer with a woman. The beautiful brunette woman next to Mickey trembled. She looked over at him, on the verge of tears.

"I'm gonna need to hold your hand, Mick, or I swear to you I'll fall down."

"I won't let you," Mickey said, and took her hand.

He walked with her resolutely until they found the room number they'd been given at reception, and stopped. The door was closed.

"You want me to go in first?" he asked.

She shook her head. "It has to be me. He's expecting me."

She fumbled in her purse, came up with a nip bottle of vodka she'd bought in the duty-free shop, and twisted off the cap.

"You don't need that."

"Oh yes I do," she said, and drank it down.

Dropping the empty in her purse, she turned the handle and pushed open the door into a room that held a single patient lying in bed and facing a screen showing CNN. He was in a body cast with a neck halo. Bandages swathed his head. His left arm was gone. Both lower legs were missing above the knee. His eyes were closed.

"Hawkes?" she said in a quavering voice. "It's me."

ERNEST MORRIS

The man inside the bandages opened his eyes and rolled them her way. "Deb?" He grunted it more than said it. His jaw was wired shut.

Deb started crying. Shoulders hunched, clutching her purse like a life preserver, she moved uncertainly toward the foot of the bed, where Hawkes could see her better.

"I'm right here, baby. So is Mickey."

Mickey came into the room, feeling more frightened than anything. He waved at the legless creature inside the bandages and said hi.

Hawkes screamed, "Get him out! I told you not to bring him! Get him out, Deb!"

"But he's—"

"Get him out!" Hawkes screeched. Monitors began to buzz and whine in alarm.

Shocked and feeling rejected, Mickey started toward the door. Then the tears came and his

168

own anger flared. He spun and shouted, "Why didn't you leave when you said you would? You left when you said you would, and we never would have been blown up! Never!"

Somebody nudged him. Mickey jerked awake, realized he'd been yelling in his sleep. He looked around and saw a kindly older man with a cane.

"Nightmare, son?" the old man said.

Mickey nodded, realizing how sweaty he felt under the windbreaker, the hoodie, and the vest, and then how close he was to his stop. Glancing past the older man, he scanned a woman reading a magazine while the six or seven other passengers at the far back of the bus stared off into space with work-glazed expressions.

"Time to really wake them up," Mickey said out loud when the bus pulled over across from

Veterans Affairs Medical Center. "This soldier's done fooling around."

Already late and not wanting to miss any more of the evening meeting, Mickey got up, waited until the rear doors opened with a whoosh, and hurried off the bus. He didn't notice that the woman reading the magazine was now staring after him. He didn't look back to see her get off the bus and trail him at a distance.

# Chapter 22

Shayana, Le'Shea, and I were waiting on my grandmother to finish some last-minute dinner preparations, when my cell phone rang.

"Don't you dare," my grandmother said, shaking a wooden spoon at me. "I've been working on this meal since noon."

I held up my hands in surrender, let the call go to voicemail, and sniffed at delicious odors seeping out from under the lid of a large deep-sided pan.

"Smells great, Grandmom!" Shayana said, reaching for the lid.

She gave him a gentle fanny swat with the spoon.

"No peeking behind curtain number one."

My cell rang again, prompting a disapproving sniff from my grandmother. I pulled out the phone, expecting Sharon to be calling. We had all been frustrated leaving Vincente's apartment earlier in the day. He'd looked good for the bomber going in, and not so good coming out. He seemed even more unlikely when Metro transit confirmed he'd never once ridden the Circulator, and the US Army confirmed he'd been a cook. But it wasn't Sharon on my caller ID. Kate Williams was looking for me.

"Dinner in five minutes," my grandmother said.

I walked out into the front hall. "Kate?"

"I think I've got him, Dr. Morris," she said breathlessly. "I'm sitting on the bomber."

"What? Where?"

"Veteran's Affair Medical Center. He's in a support group meeting for IED-wounded vets until seven fifty. I figure you have until eight to meet me at the bus stop at Brookland–CUA."

The call ended. I stared at the phone. My grandmother called out.

"I'm sorry, Gram," I said, grabbing my raincoat. "I've gotta go."

Out the door and down the front stairs, I ran north in the pouring rain to Pennsylvania Avenue and hailed a cab. On the way I tried to reach Sharon, but it kept going through to her voicemail. I texted her what Kate had said and that I was going to check it out. As smart and IED savvy as my patient was, I wasn't holding out real hope that she'd somehow identified the bomber. But I wasn't going to ignore her either.

In the rain, traffic was snarled, so I didn't climb out of a cab at the Brookland–CUA Metro Station until two minutes past eight. Kate Williams stood at the bus stop shelter, leaning against a Plexiglass wall, smoking a cigarette and perusing *People* magazine.

Seeing me, she stubbed the butt out, flipped it into a trash can, and smiled.

"Means a lot that you came," she said. She explained that she'd come back looking for me the night before and saw me in the D8 bus talking to Mr. Jacobs.

Kate put two and two together and spent most of the day riding the Circulator and the Hospital Center bus lines. Around six, she got on the Hospital Center bus at Union Station and saw a guy she recognized, sleeping in a seat near the back.

"I didn't think much of him, beyond the fact that I'd seen him down around the Vietnam Memorial before," she said. "But when we got close to the hospital, he had some kind of nightmare and yelled out something about getting blown up."

"I'm sure there are lots of guys who ride this

bus and have flashbacks."

"I'm sure they do," she said. "But they don't wear a blue rain jacket with a logo on the left chest that says . . . shit, here he comes. Half a block. Don't look. Put your hood up. If he's been watching the news, he'll recognize you."

The D8 bus pulled in.

"Get on before he does," Kate said. "You'll be behind him. Easier to control."

Chapter 23

I hesitated, but only for a beat. If it really was the bomber, being positioned behind him could be a good thing, especially in a confined space. I pivoted away and climbed aboard. Gordon Jacob was driving. He recognized me and started to say something, but I held a finger to my lips as I ran my Metro card over the reader.

I headed toward the rear of the semi-crowded bus but stood instead of taking a seat, holding on to a strap facing the side windows. When the doors shut and we started to move, I lowered my hood and glanced around.

Kate was standing in the aisle ten feet forward of me. Her eyes met mine, and she slightly tilted her head toward a man wearing a dark blue windbreaker, hood up. He was looking out the window, giving me no view of his face. The seat beside him was empty. So was the entire seat behind him.

Kate sat next to him, blocking his exit, which caused him to pivot his head to glance at her. "What the hell is she thinking?" I groaned to myself. And what the hell was I thinking, coming on this wild goose chase?

Because I could now see that under a mop of frizzy brown hair was a bored, pimply, teenage boy, who turned away from Kate when she opened her magazine. Her right hand left the magazine and gestured behind her at the empty seat.

I wanted to get off at the next exit and head home. Maybe Grandmom had saved me a plate. But when the bus slowed for a red light, I thought, "What the hell?" Kate had led me this far. I slipped into the seat behind them. When the bus started rolling again, Kate shut her magazine.

"I have a friend who goes to your school."

I kept a neutral expression. The kid didn't respond at first, then looked over at her.

"What's that?" he said, roused from thought.

"Benjamin Banneker High School," she said. "It's on your jacket."

"Oh," he said, without enthusiasm. "Yeah."

"She runs track. Le'Shea Morris. You know her?"

The kid gave her a sidelong glance. "She's in my chemistry class."

Chemistry and in Le'Shea's class. Now I was interested. Real interested.

"Nice girl, that Le'Shea," Kate said. "What's your name so I can tell her I met you?"

He hesitated, but then answered, "Mickey. Mickey Hawkes."

"Kate Williams. Nice to meet you, Mickey Hawkes," she said, and smiled.

We pulled over at a bus stop, and more people started to board. Kate spoke.

"Must have been scary there for a while yesterday."

"Scary?" Mickey said.

"You know. The bomb threat?"

His posture stiffened.

"Oh, that. It was more boring than scary. We stood there for hours, waiting to see the school explode. I should have gone home."

"So you were out there the entire time?"

"Yup. Like three solid hours."

"Huh," Kate said. She looked at him directly. "Mickey, it's weird. I'm one of these people who remembers every face they see. And I distinctly remember seeing you come off the Circulator bus at the Vietnam Memorial, maybe twenty minutes after the school was evacuated."

"What? No."

"Yes. You were wearing that same wind-breaker. You were excited and looking at your cell phone. Probably at the news that school had been evacuated after you called Le'Shea Morris with the bomb threat."

The kid looked up for two long beats before turning fully toward her. He looked past her, over his shoulder to me. In a split second I saw recognition, fear, and resolution in his expression. This was our guy, but he was just a kid. Twisting away from us, he lurched to his feet and stepped onto his seat, holding his cell phone high overhead.

"I'm wearing a bomb vest!" he shouted. "Do what I say, or everyone dies!"

~ ~ ~

Passengers began to scream and scramble

away from Mickey.

"Shut up and don't move!" the teen yelled, shaking the cell phone at them. "Everyone shut up and sit down, or will kill us all right now!"

The few passengers on their feet slowly sank into seats, and the bus quieted, save for a few frightened whimpers.

"Good," the teenager said, and then called to Gordon Jacobs. "No more stops, driver. Straight south now."

I wished I had a gun. Lacking that, I eased my phone from my coat pocket.

"Where are we going?" Kate Williams asked.

"You'll see," Mickey said, his head swiveling all around.

He looked at me, then back toward the front. When he did, I moved my hands and phone forward toward the back of his seat where I hoped he couldn't see them. The second time his head swung away from me, I glanced down to text Sharon and Mahogany: "Bomber taken D-8 bus hostage. Headed south on—" I punched 911 into my phone.

"I can't!" Gordon yelled. "It's one way there!"

"911, what is your emergency?" I heard the woman say.

The driver slammed on his brakes and cut right through a small parking area off Mass Avenue. The bus hit a curb with a jolt. People screamed. My chin hit the back of Kate's seat, and I dropped my phone, which went skittering across the floor before the bus smashed down onto Northwest Drive along the boundary of the Capitol's grounds.

I was dazed for a moment, hearing cars honking and swerving to get out of the way of the bus, which went careening uphill. As I shook off the daze, Mickey moved forward toward Gordon Jacob, his cell phone held high. Passengers shrank from him as he advanced, yelling.

"Turn on the lights in here. Open your window. And take the next right, Driver. Go right on up to the barrier!"

"The next right? I can't! It's—"

"Do it!"

Mickey ran up beside the driver. Jacob glanced at the cell phone Mickey held, before pressing a button that opened his window, and another that lit up the interior of the bus. He downshifted and swung the bus right, following the curve of a short spur road that led to a bunker-like guard shack and a solid steel gate.

Ahead, through the windshield, I could see the lights of satellite media trucks blazing across the small plaza in front of the steps of the

Senate. A Capitol Hill Police officer armed with an H&K submachine gun stepped out of the shack.

"What the hell are you doing!" she shouted at Gordon. "Back the hell up! This is a restri-cted—"

"I'm wearing a bomb!" Mickey Hawkes yelled. "And I'm going to explode it and kill you and all these people unless I get to talk to those senators. Right here. Right now."

I recognized the officer; her last name was Carson. She hesitated until Mikey exposed the bomb vest again.

"Do it," Mickey said. "Call in there. And don't even think of trying to shoot me. I drop this phone, the IED goes off."

Officer Carson blinked and said, "Let's calm down a second here, son. I can't just call into the Senate. I wouldn't even know how."

"Bullshit."

"She's right, Mickey Hawkes," I called loudly, and got up.

He looked at me as I started past Kate. "Sit down, man."

I hesitated. Kate tugged on my pants leg. I looked down at her and saw she wanted to tell me something.

"What?"

She glanced at Mickey and said, "Nothing."

Mickey had turned to the Capitol Hill cop.

"Call your boss, lady, or call his boss. I'm sure one of them knows how to contact the senators blocking the vet's bill."

"Is that what this is about?" I said, moving up the aisle.

"Sit down, or I blow this now!" he shouted at me.

I sat down seven rows from the front with

my hands up. Mickey looked back at Officer Carson, who hadn't moved since.

"Call now!" he yelled. "Or do you want to explain how you could have stopped the bloodbath that's about to happen?"

Carson held up a hand and said, "Calm down, and I'll try to make the call."

"Mickey, how about letting some of these people go while she tries?" I asked.

He glared at me. "Why would I do that?"

"To show your goodwill."

"There's no such thing as goodwill," Mickey said. "Why do you think I'm here?"

Carson backed through the door into the guard shack.

"Mickey, why are you here?" I said.

"I'll tell those senators."

"You could start with us," I said. "Convince us, maybe you convince them."

The teenager didn't look at me, but I could see him struggle. He said, "I'm saying this once, my way."

"You could—"

"Shut up, Dr. Morris!" he shouted. "I know what you're trying to do! I've seen what all you goddamned shrinks try to do!"

Officer Carson emerged from the security bunker. I looked out the windows and saw the silhouettes of armed officers racing from all directions to surround the bus.

"Mickey, I can't call the senators," she said.

"You can't?" he screamed. "Or you won't?"

"I don't make these kinds of calls, Mickey," she replied. "But there's no way we're going to let a senator anywhere near you and your bomb."

His jaw clenched. He looked out the wind-shield, and back at the cop.

ERNEST MORRIS

"Get them on the Senate steps then. And give me a bullhorn."

Carson started to shake her head, but I intervened and yelled, "Call, Officer. See if it's possible."

I was standing again. Carson could see me through the windows. She hesitated, but then nodded.

"I'll ask, Dr. Morris." She disappeared back inside the bunker.

"If you get your chance to talk to them, Mickey, you'll let us go?"

He shook his head and said, "I want to see some action."

Before I could reply, Carson exited the bunker again. "I'm sorry, Mickey, but they won't allow it."

His jaw tensed again as he struggled for another option. But then he straightened and gave Carson a sorry look.

"I guess I have to make a different kind of statement then, don't I?" He held up the cell phone and looked back at me. "Sorry I had to hack into Le'Shea's phone, Dr. Morris. I always liked her."

I saw flickers of anger, fear, and despair on his face. I'd seen the same in Kate Williams's face when we first met. I understood he was suicidal.

"Don't, Mickey!" I said.

"Too late," Mickey replied. He moved his thumb to the screen.

# Chapter 24

There was a flash of brilliant light, and I started to duck, but then I saw it was behind Mickey. For a moment the kid was silhouetted there. I felt sure there would be a blast. We were going to die. Then Kate Williams stood and yelled.

"The bullhorn's behind you, Mickey!"

The teen looked confused, then glanced over his shoulder through the windshield. There were news cameramen running toward the bus, klieg lights flaring in the rain, and satellite trucks following.

"Go, Mickey!" Kate shouted. "Before they figure it out!"

Mickey stared at her as they shared an understanding that eluded me, then addressed Gordon Jacob.

"Open the door!"

The driver pushed a button. The front and rear doors whooshed open. Mickey looked at us.

"Sorry it had to come to this."

He climbed out. I waited two seconds before I ran forward.

"Everyone out the back, and move away, now."

The other passengers lunged for the rear exit. I went out the front door and watched Mickey Hawkes go toward the barrier that blocked access to the Capitol, his jacket open, exposing the vest. Officer Carson was aiming her rifle at him.

"Not a step further, Mickey."

He stopped at the thick, solid steel barrier, which came up to the bottom of the vest, and stood there squinting as the cameras and lights came within yards and formed in a ragged semicircle facing him. Kate climbed from the bus and stood by me.

"You should get out of here," I said.

"No," she said. "It's all right."

"Who are you?" one of the journalists shouted.

"What do you want to tell the senators?" another cried.

We watched silently, transfixed. Mickey put one hand on the bomb vest and showed them the cell phone with the other.

"My name is Michael Hawkes," he said in a wavering, emotional voice. "I am seventeen years old. When I was eight, my father, my hero and my best friend, was blown up by an IED on his ride back to Kabul to muster out of the Special Forces for good."

"Shit," Kate said under her breath.

"Maybe he should have died," Mickey went

on. "Most of the time he says he should have. He lost both legs and an arm and suffered a closed head injury. When I went with my mother to see him at the hospital in Germany, he wouldn't let me into his room."

His shoulders heaved, and I knew he was crying.

"My dad said to forget him. He told my mom the same thing. But I wouldn't forget my dad. No matter how many times he swore at me, no matter how many times he told me to never come back, I went to see him in every hospital he's lived in since the explosion."

Mickey paused and looked around at Officer Carson, who had lowered her gun. He glanced over at us. I nodded.

"Keep going. You're doing fine," Kate said.

"I finally started to get through to my dad two years ago," Mikey said, turning back to the cameras. "There are daily support group meet-ings for IED survivors and their families at Veterans Affairs Medical Center. I go every day I can because I want to be there for my father and because it's the only way I really get to see him when he doesn't get angry, and it's the only way he stays sane, and—." His voice cracked as he said, "If I don't—."

Mickey looked at the sky, coughed, and cleared his throat before pointing toward the Senate.

"The politicians in there owe my dad," he said. "They made a promise that if he risked his life for his nation, his nation would stand by him. They made a promise that his nation would not forget him that his grateful nation would help and provide for him."

Mickey took a deep breath and continued his rant.

"But those senators in there aren't standing by their promises, and they're not standing by my father. They've forgotten him, and every other vet. They've forgotten to be grateful to those who served. If they don't pass this bill tonight, the funding for veterans stops. The VA hospitals shut down. The programs halt. The help my dad needs is gone. The help every wounded warrior in the country needs is gone. And I— I can't let that happen."

He paused and then said in a strong voice, "Pass the bill, senators, or I'll blow myself up, and the blood's on your hands."

# Chapter 25

The rain picked up. So did the wind. And so did the pressure on Mickey Hawkes to give up his demands and surrender. But Mickey stood resolute at the gate, holding his cell phone and staring beyond the cameras at the lights burning over the steps of the Senate. I didn't like his tactics a bit, and yet the more I watched him, the more I admired his guts and conviction.

Sharon arrived ten minutes into the standoff, Ned Mahogany a few minutes later. She'd watched Mickey's speech streaming on her phone and told us the cable news networks were going crazy with the story. It was irresistible, a David versus Goliath showdown, the teen versus Congress.

"What can we do?" she asked, peeking around me to look at Mickey.

"We can wait him out," I said. "There's been no vote yet."

Mickey's mother, Deborah Hawkes, a disheveled-looking woman in her early forties, arrived on the scene shortly after nine, climbing from a patrol car that had been dispatched to her apartment blocks away. She appeared not only frantic, but also possibly drunk.

"Mick!" she yelled when Ned Mahogany led her up alongside the bus. "Oh my God! What the hell do you think you're doing?"

He ignored her.

"Mickey!" she shouted. "You answer me."

The teen never turned toward her. "I'm doing what you wouldn't, Ma. I'm helping Dad, and every vet like him."

She started to sob quietly. "He left me," she said. "He left you too."

"I wouldn't let him leave me," Mickey said.

197

"That's the difference between us."

The cameras caught all of it. According to the live updates Sharon was watching, the phones in the senators' offices were ringing off the hook with calls from vets and families, urging them to pass the bill. Apparently Mickey's threat was echoing in the Senate. For supporters of the bill, he was the dramatic proof they needed to argue that lack of support for veterans had gone too far.

The senators opposed to passage called Mickey a terrorist and a blackmailer.

"They do this after every big war, you know," Mickey shouted at the cameras around 10:00 p.m. "Congress gets all gung ho to spend to fight. But when it's time to take care of the vets, they claim poverty because of how much they spent on the war. It happened after the Revolutionary War, the Civil War, World War I, and

World War II.

"The Vietnam vets? They got screwed too. So did the ones who fought in Desert Storm. And now it's happening all over again for the soldiers who served in Iraq and Afghanistan. When is this going to stop? When are they going to fulfill their promises?"

A cheer went up from behind the bus, back out on Northeast Drive where a crowd, many of them veterans, it seemed, had gathered to lend Mickey support.

At 10:20, we heard that debate over the veteran's bill had been closed. An up or down vote was underway. Fifteen minutes after that, with the ongoing vote leaning 44–40 against passage, a panel van parked on Northeast Drive. Thomas Hawkes rolled out the back in a motorized wheelchair. Officer Carson led him around the security bunker, lowered the steel barrier, and let Hawkes wheel toward his son.

"Jesus, Mickey," Hawkes said. "You sure know how to cause a shit storm."

Mickey smiled, but his jaw was trembling. "I learned from the best."

"No, son, I think you've got me beat by a long shot."

Mickey didn't reply.

"You gonna blow yourself up?"

A long moment passed before Mickey answered.

"If I have to."

Hawkes looked pained and used his remaining arm to bring his wheelchair closer.

"I don't want you to," he said, quiet but forceful. "I want you to stay in this world. And— I'm sorry for all the times I pushed you away. I need you, Mick."

Mickey started crying again, but stood still.

"You hear me?" his father said. "The whole goddamned world needs men like you, willing to take a stand. A warrior if there ever was one."

Back by the road, claps and whistles of approval went up from the crowd, many of whom were also watching live updates on their smartphones. Mickey wiped at his tears and looked over his shoulder at Kate Williams, who shook her head ever so slightly.

"Give up, Mick," his mother called. "I promise. I'll be better. We'll be better."

"Listen to her," Hawkes said. "We both need you in our lives. And we both can change things, if you'll just—"

Suddenly a shout rang out from one of the broadcast journalists.

"Passed! It passed by two votes!"

"You did it, Mickey!"

The kid hung his head and leaned on the

barrier, sobbing. His father wheeled toward him while his mother tried to get around Mahogany, who held her back.

"Not until my people have defused that vest," he said.

"Don't worry about it," Kate said, wiping tears from her eyes. "There's no bomb."

Sharon, Mahogany, and I all said in unison, "What?"

"Sorry, Doc," she said, laughing and shaking her head. "I know a real IED when I see one, and I knew right away he was wearing a fake. That hot-shit, nerves-of-steel kid just bluffed the whole goddamned thing!"

## Epilogue

Two weeks later, in the early evening, I was helping my grandmother set the table for six. The aromas wafting from the oven were heavenly. Painfully hungry, I wished I'd eaten a bigger lunch.

"What time did you say dinner was?" my grandmother said.

"Six thirty."

My grandmother nodded and checked her watch. It was just shy of six. "That'll be fine then. I'll start the jasmine rice, and you can finish up here?"

"Seeing how you put this together on short notice, I'd be happy to."

That pleased her. She opened the oven to take a peek at the lamb shanks, bone-in, braising in the oven. It smelled so good my stomach growled.

"I heard that," Sharon said, and laughed as she came into the kitchen.

"The whole neighborhood heard it," Grand-mom chuckled.

"It's your fault," I said. "My stomach's just reacting to your latest masterpiece."

That pleased her even more. I saw her smile as she put the rice into a cooker. Sharon gave me a kiss and picked up the napkins.

"Good day?" I said.

She thought about it and said, "Yeah, you know, it was. The pressure was off, and I could think about something other than the bomber."

"Mickey's story shaking out?"

Sharon cocked her head and pursed her lips, but nodded.

"So far, but he broke about fifty different laws. He can't get around that, even if he is a juvenile."

"They're making him sound awful sympa-
thetic in the media," I said.

She shrugged. "They're focused on the
mitigating circumstances."

"What does that mean?" my grandmother
asked.

Sharon explained the latest: Mickey Hawkes
had cooperated fully since his arrest. Kate
Williams had been absolutely right that there
was no bomb in his vest. The "plastic explosive
blocks" he carried were actually large chunks of
colored wax.

The wiring was nonsensical, connected to no
timer or triggering device whatsoever. Kate had
recognized the wiring issues immediately, but
wanted to see what Mickey was going to do with
a fake vest.

Once the veteran's bill had passed the

Senate, bound for the president's desk, Mickey Hawkes had surrendered. As he was led off the Capitol grounds in handcuffs, the crowd of vets on Constitution Avenue and Northeast Drive broke into cheers and applause.

"I watch the news. He's got popular opinion on his side," my grandmother allowed. "But he did set off three bombs, and that plastic explosive at the Korean Memorial. And he did blackmail the Senate."

She wasn't wrong, but it wasn't the whole story. It turned out that the bombs on the Mall were made from muzzleloader black powder, tamped into thick cardboard tubes and wrapped in duct tape. With no ball bearings or screws inside, they were basically large firecrackers.

Mickey had told Ned Mahogany that he found the small chunk of plastic explosive material buried in a locker sent back from US Special

Forces in Afghanistan, shortly after the IED explosion that took his father's arm and legs.

Mickey had done enough research to know that the small amount of C-4 could not do any significant damage, so he decided to leave it at the Korean Memorial to raise the stakes, making us believe he had access to unscented plastic explosives. My grandmother seemed unconvinced.

"We were stumped on this, too, Grandmom," Sharon said.

"But you have to hand it to him," I said. "He actually got Congress to act."

"Pigs fly every once and a while," my grandmother said.

"What?" Shayana said, looking puzzled as she came into the kitchen. "They do not."

"It's just an expression," sighed Le'Shea, who followed her, looking at her phone mid texting. "It means that miracles can happen."

The doorbell rang.

"I'll get it," I said, pausing to give Le'Shea a hug. "No phones at the table. No phones behind the wheel."

She scrunched up her nose but put her phone in her pocket. "A deal's a deal."

"Thank you for remembering," I said, and gave her a kiss on the cheek.

"I can't believe she's getting a car just for controlling her texting," Shayana said.

As I was leaving the kitchen, Le'Shea said, "Maybe you'll believe it when you need a ride."

The doorbell rang again. I hustled down the front hall and opened it to Kate Williams.

"Welcome!" I said.

"Not too early?"

"Right on time. I hope you're hungry for a home-cooked meal."

"It's been a long time." Kate smiled. "It smells outstanding! I'm just happy to be invited, Dr. Morris."

"Upstairs, I'm E. J. And you do look happy."

Kate stopped in the hallway, grinning and lowering her voice.

"I probably shouldn't be telling you this, but I got a call from the lab at Quantico this morning. There's a slot open in TEDAC, the Terrorist Explosive Device Analytical Center. They want me to interview for it!"

"Wow. That is great news! How did that happen?"

"I'm not sure. Maybe your friend? Agent Mahogany?"

"I'll ask him if you want."

"No, no, it doesn't matter. I'm just—I can see a way forward now, Dr. — E. J., and I'm grateful."

"You deserve it. Want to meet the rest of my family?"

"I'd like that. But, I wanted to say thank you. For all the help you've given me."

"Glad I could help, Kate," I said. I smiled and gestured toward the kitchen.

Following her, remembering the near-suicidal woman who'd sat down in my office not two weeks before, I couldn't help thinking that maybe that suspension wasn't such a bad thing. Sometimes miracles really do happen.

"Hello," said grandmom. "Have a seat."

Everyone sat down at the table so that they could enjoy some of the best food around. I introduced everyone to Kate. They all spoke, then dug into their plates of food. As we ate and conversed about different topics, Sharon's phone started buzzing. She ignored it. Ten seconds later, it began buzzing again. Normally we wouldn't answer any calls while at the table, but this was different. It was her boss.

"Chief Probes, what can I do for you, sir?" she said in an aggravated tone.

"We have a serious problem, Sharon. Go to your window and take a look."

Sharon got up from the table in a hurry. I looked at her heading toward the living room and followed behind her.

"What is it?" I asked, walking up beside her as she pulled the curtain to the side.

"Oh my God," she said with her hand over her mouth.

When I looked out the window, two buildings were in flames, and a third blew up seconds later. I watched, just as shocked as Sharon was.

"Get your ass downtown now. Shit has just hit the fan, again," he stated, then ended the call.

## About The Author

Ernest E. J. Morris has created more enduring fictional characters than he could count. He is the author of the Flipping Numbers and Naughty Housewives series, which are two of his most popular series today. Some of his other novels include:

*Trapped in Love, Supreme and Justice, Deadly Reunion, A Hustler's Dream, Killing Signs, Money Makes Me Cum, Black Reign, Lost and Turned Out, Forbidden Passion, The Betrayal Within, Death by Association, Can't Knock the Hustle, The Game Don't Love You, The Webpage Murders, Me and Karma, Her Double Life,* and *The Infirmary.*

Coming Soon: *A Nurse's Betrayal.*

Ernest Morris has also written a book called *Breaking the Chains,* which focuses on teaching young kids how to stay out of trouble. He shares his own life experiences, with the hopes of saving the next generation. His life-long passion for writing has helped him through good and bad times. He writes full-time and lives in Pennsylvania.

If you would like to contact him, you can follow him on Facebook at EJMORRIS or Instagram at EJFLIPPIN, or you can email him at EJMORRIS54@gmail.com.

*To order books, please fill out the order form below:*
*To order films please go to www.good2gofilms.com*

Name:_____
Address:_____
City:_____State:_____Zip Code: _____
Phone:_____
Email:_____
Method of Payment:     Check      VISA  MASTERCARD
Credit Card#:_ _____
Name as it appears on card: _____
Signature: _____

| Item Name | Price | Qty | Amount |
|---|---|---|---|
| 48 Hours to Die – Silk White | $14.99 | | |
| A Hustler's Dream – Ernest Morris | $14.99 | | |
| A Hustler's Dream 2 – Ernest Morris | $14.99 | | |
| A Thug's Devotion – J. L. Rose and J. M. McMillon | $14.99 | | |
| All Eyes on Tommy Gunz – Warren Holloway | $14.99 | | |
| Black Reign – Ernest Morris | $14.99 | | |
| Bloody Mayhem Down South – Trayvon Jackson | $14.99 | | |
| Bloody Mayhem Down South 2 – Trayvon Jackson | $14.99 | | |
| Business Is Business – Silk White | $14.99 | | |
| Business Is Business 2 – Silk White | $14.99 | | |
| Business Is Business 3 – Silk White | $14.99 | | |
| Cash In Cash Out – Assa Raymond Baker | $14.99 | | |
| Cash In Cash Out 2 – Assa Raymond Baker | $14.99 | | |
| Childhood Sweethearts – Jacob Spears | $14.99 | | |
| Childhood Sweethearts 2 – Jacob Spears | $14.99 | | |
| Childhood Sweethearts 3 – Jacob Spears | $14.99 | | |
| Childhood Sweethearts 4 – Jacob Spears | $14.99 | | |
| Connected To The Plug – Dwan Marquis Williams | $14.99 | | |
| Connected To The Plug 2 – Dwan Marquis Williams | $14.99 | | |
| Connected To The Plug 3 – Dwan Williams | $14.99 | | |
| Cost of Betrayal – W.C. Holloway | $14.99 | | |
| Cost of Betrayal 2 – W.C. Holloway | $14.99 | | |
| Deadly Reunion – Ernest Morris | $14.99 | | |
| Dream's Life – Assa Raymond Baker | $14.99 | | |
| Flipping Numbers – Ernest Morris | $14.99 | | |
| Flipping Numbers 2 – Ernest Morris | $14.99 | | |

| | | | |
|---|---|---|---|
| Forbidden Pleasure – Ernest Morris | $14.99 | | |
| He Loves Me, He Loves You Not – Mychea | $14.99 | | |
| He Loves Me, He Loves You Not 2 – Mychea | $14.99 | | |
| He Loves Me, He Loves You Not 3 – Mychea | $14.99 | | |
| He Loves Me, He Loves You Not 4 – Mychea | $14.99 | | |
| He Loves Me, He Loves You Not 5 – Mychea | $14.99 | | |
| Killing Signs – Ernest Morris | $14.99 | | |
| Killing Signs 2 – Ernest Morris | $14.99 | | |
| Kings of the Block – Dwan Willams | $14.99 | | |
| Kings of the Block 2 – Dwan Willams | $14.99 | | |
| Lord of My Land – Jay Morrison | $14.99 | | |
| Lost and Turned Out – Ernest Morris | $14.99 | | |
| Love & Dedication – W.C. Holloway | $14.99 | | |
| Love Hates Violence – De'Wayne Maris | $14.99 | | |
| Love Hates Violence 2 – De'Wayne Maris | $14.99 | | |
| Love Hates Violence 3 – De'Wayne Maris | $14.99 | | |
| Love Hates Violence 4 – De'Wayne Maris | $14.99 | | |
| Married To Da Streets – Silk White | $14.99 | | |
| M.E.R.C. – Make Every Rep Count Health and Fitness | $14.99 | | |
| Mercenary In Love – J.L. Rose & J.L. Turner | $14.99 | | |
| Money Make Me Cum – Ernest Morris | $14.99 | | |
| My Besties – Asia Hill | $14.99 | | |
| My Besties 2 – Asia Hill | $14.99 | | |
| My Besties 3 – Asia Hill | $14.99 | | |
| My Besties 4 – Asia Hill | $14.99 | | |
| My Boyfriend's Wife – Mychea | $14.99 | | |
| My Boyfriend's Wife 2 – Mychea | $14.99 | | |
| My Brothers Envy – J. L. Rose | $14.99 | | |
| My Brothers Envy 2 – J. L. Rose | $14.99 | | |
| Naughty Housewives – Ernest Morris | $14.99 | | |
| Naughty Housewives 2 – Ernest Morris | $14.99 | | |
| Naughty Housewives 3 – Ernest Morris | $14.99 | | |
| Naughty Housewives 4 – Ernest Morris | $14.99 | | |
| Never Be The Same – Silk White | $14.99 | | |
| Scarred Faces – Assa Raymond Baker | $14.99 | | |

| | | | |
|---|---|---|---|
| Scarred Knuckles – Assa Raymond Baker | $14.99 | | |
| Secrets in the Dark – Ernest Morris | $14.99 | | |
| Shades of Revenge – Assa Raymond Baker | $14.99 | | |
| Slumped – Jason Brent | $14.99 | | |
| Someone's Gonna Get It – Mychea | $14.99 | | |
| Stranded – Silk White | $14.99 | | |
| Supreme & Justice – Ernest Morris | $14.99 | | |
| Supreme & Justice 2 – Ernest Morris | $14.99 | | |
| Supreme & Justice 3 – Ernest Morris | $14.99 | | |
| Tears of a Hustler – Silk White | $14.99 | | |
| Tears of a Hustler 2 – Silk White | $14.99 | | |
| Tears of a Hustler 3 – Silk White | $14.99 | | |
| Tears of a Hustler 4 – Silk White | $14.99 | | |
| Tears of a Hustler 5 – Silk White | $14.99 | | |
| Tears of a Hustler 6 – Silk White | $14.99 | | |
| The Betrayal Within – Ernest Morris | $14.99 | | |
| The Danger That Lurks Within – Ernest Morris | $14.99 | | |
| The Last Love Letter – Warren Holloway | $14.99 | | |
| The Last Love Letter 2 – Warren Holloway | $14.99 | | |
| The Panty Ripper – Reality Way | $14.99 | | |
| The Panty Ripper 3 – Reality Way | $14.99 | | |
| The Solution – Jay Morrison | $14.99 | | |
| The Teflon Queen – Silk White | $14.99 | | |
| The Teflon Queen 2 – Silk White | $14.99 | | |
| The Teflon Queen 3 – Silk White | $14.99 | | |
| The Teflon Queen 4 – Silk White | $14.99 | | |
| The Teflon Queen 5 – Silk White | $14.99 | | |
| The Teflon Queen 6 – Silk White | $14.99 | | |
| The Vacation – Silk White | $14.99 | | |
| The Webpage Murder – Ernest Morris | $14.99 | | |
| The Webpage Murder 2 – Ernest Morris | $14.99 | | |
| Tied To A Boss – J.L. Rose | $14.99 | | |
| Tied To A Boss 2 – J.L. Rose | $14.99 | | |
| Tied To A Boss 3 – J.L. Rose | $14.99 | | |
| Tied To A Boss 4 – J.L. Rose | $14.99 | | |
| Tied To A Boss 5 – J.L. Rose | $14.99 | | |

| | | | |
|---|---|---|---|
| Time Is Money – Silk White | $14.99 | | |
| Tomorrow's Not Promised – Robert Torres | $14.99 | | |
| Tomorrow's Not Promised 2 – Robert Torres | $14.99 | | |
| Two Mask One Heart – Jacob Spears and Trayvon Jackson | $14.99 | | |
| Two Mask One Heart 2 – Jacob Spears and Trayvon Jackson | $14.99 | | |
| Two Mask One Heart 3 – Jacob Spears and Trayvon Jackson | $14.99 | | |
| Wife – Assa Ray Baker & Raneissa Baker | $14.99 | | |
| Wife 2 – Assa Ray Baker & Raneissa Baker | $14.99 | | |
| Wrong Place Wrong Time – Silk White | $14.99 | | |
| Young Goonz – Reality Way | $14.99 | | |
| | | | |
| Subtotal: | | | |
| Tax: | | | |
| Shipping (Free) U.S. Media Mail: | | | |
| Total: | | | |

**Make Checks Payable to Good2Go Publishing, 7311 W Glass Lane, Laveen, AZ 85339**

CPSIA information can be obtained
at www.ICGtesting.com
Printed in the USA
LVHW051758191121
703844LV00017B/1392